BEAUTIFUL BURN

Hill City Heroes, Book Two

RACHEL BLAKE

Published by Blushing Books
An Imprint of
ABCD Graphics and Design, Inc.
A Virginia Corporation
977 Seminole Trail #233
Charlottesville, VA 22901

Rachel Blake
Beautiful Burn

EBook ISBN: 978-1-948045-21-6
Print ISBN: 978-1-64563-180-4
v1

Cover Art by ABCD Graphics & Design

Chapter 1

Gwendolyn stared at her reflection in the smudged mirror. Her auburn hair was pulled back into a long ponytail at the crown of her head, and she eyed the strands already trying to escape the confines of the elastic band. Her curls had a mind of their own and she knew that in just a few short hours, she would have a head full of frizz despite her efforts to tame the locks.

The sound of the heavy locker room door opening stopped the scrutiny of herself, but it was the sound of hot and heavy kissing that forced the exaggerated sigh from her lips. "Seriously! You could at least do a sweep of the room first."

"Sorry, Gwen." Leland's apology was torn to shreds when the sound of Autumn's laughter hit Gwen's ears. "Princess." Gwen smiled when she heard the muttered ow from the other side of the room.

"We agreed you wouldn't call me that at work."

"*I* agreed to nothing. And if you pinch me again, I will drag you to the repair closet again."

With one more quick glance at herself, Gwen headed toward the door and the overly enthusiastic couple. "Seriously, guys, you were literally apart, what, maybe an hour this morning? Do you have to start with the groping so early?" She paused in her turn toward the door. "Oh, and do us all a favor and move in together already. Having to pretend we don't know you guys spent the night together is starting to get old."

"I told you we weren't fooling anyone, princess."

Gwen watched as her partner glowered at the man, earning herself a pinch to the thigh. "Come on, *princess*, let's get the rig check done before you get yourself into any more trouble."

"See! That is why you need to stop calling me that at work." The man simply raised an eyebrow and shook his head. As soon as they were in the hallway, Autumn started whispering, "That was the worst hint you could have *ever* given. He knew the second you spoke that I put you up to it."

"He's your Dom. Isn't the first rule of your relationship something about communication?"

Autumn rolled her eyes. "Only about the important stuff."

"I doubt he would agree with that statement." When they arrived at the ambulance, Gwen turned to her friend. "Just tell him that you want to move in. You guys have been through more in your six months together than most have in their entire life. You belong together, and you both know it."

"I know, but why hasn't *he* asked me to move in? I'll be damned if I am going to do it all myself."

"That is exactly why you need to talk to him. Quit beating around the bush and *tell* him what you want."

"Are you sure you're not a Domme? You have the bossy thing down. No? Then you should really stop rolling your eyes. What? I'm just trying to help you. It's going to be a hard habit to break when you finally snag yourself a Dom. See! Right there, you rolled them again!"

"Meeting in the great room. Thirty minutes," Jensen announced as he stuck his head in the back of the rig an hour later.

"He's back," Autumn stated. Her eyes narrowed as her face reddened with anger.

Gwen watched as Jensen softened the slightest bit. "You don't have to be here. No one would think less of you if you decided to pursue a different career."

"I will be damned if I am going to let that bastard keep me from doing my job." She jumped from the rig, giving the man's shoulder a shove as she passed. "If you'll excuse me, I am going to find Lee."

The smile on his face as he watched the confidant woman walk out of the garage stirred a far too familiar feeling in Gwen's gut. She quickly looked down at the incomplete checklist. "You did that on purpose."

"What?"

She gave him her best 'are you kidding me' look. "You reverse psychologied your way into getting her to do exactly as you wanted her to do."

"Is psychologied a word?" At her eye roll, he shook his head and continued. "If it works and gets her to do what she was already going to do without her stressing over what she can't change, what does it hurt? Your smile could light up an entire room." She ignored his sudden change in topic and the goofy smile plastered to his face as she turned back to the clipboard. "You know, the men around here would be a lot more likely to believe you and your claim to be straight and narrow if that look didn't take over your face as often as it does."

She absently flipped through the pages, as looking the man in the eyes right then was not an option. "What look?"

"The one on your face right now."

Shocked, she quickly studied his handsome face before brushing past him as she climbed out of the rig. "There is no look."

"There is. It's in your eyes. A soft, subtle look, but there is no doubt a look."

He followed her through the bay as she ducked and weaved past the trucks. *Doesn't he have a job to do?*

"I just don't understand why you deny your need to submit. It's nothing to be ashamed of."

She stopped in her tracks and turned on the man. "I haven't denied that need since—" She looked away, not wanting any more of a reminder. "I don't deny it anymore. I just don't talk about it like everyone else around here does. Shit. Do you know how desperately I want a man to love me the way so many of the men here love their women. I want it so badly, but before everything happened, I could hardly speak in the presence of a dominant, demanding man without tying my tongue into a knot. The worst part is that I've denied it for so long, I'm not sure I know how to talk to them anymore, let alone submit."

"That's because you didn't want to talk to them." He softly chucked her under the chin, all but forcing her to raise her eyes to his. His voice growled with the next declaration, "There isn't a guy in this station who wouldn't be willing to help you fight off old habits."

She looked away before her instincts took over and she answered the question written all over his face. "I can do it on my own. I *will* do it on my own. Dropping the timid, little mouse act was harder than I would like to admit, but I did it."

He stepped closer to her and took hold of her arms. She watched as his thumb rubbed back and forth over one of her shoulders. "I have no doubt that you can absolutely do this on your own, but when you tell people of how you conquered your inhibitions, *I* want to be part of that story."

She stood there for a second, mouth agape before she finally met his eyes. "Wait. You what?"

He smiled as he ran his finger along her bottom lip. "Come on, Gwen, you can't be that surprised. We have been hitting on each other for months, but if you need more time, I'll give it to you. Let me know when you want me to be part of that story. In the meantime, I guess flirting is better than nothing."

She licked at the path his finger had taken. "You haven't been hitting on me for months. Where are you going? You can't just drop a bomb like that and then walk away! Jensen!" He simply waved at her over his shoulder and kept walking. Her foot stomp was far less effective than she intended it to be.

"At least when he walks away, you get a great view of his best asset." Autumn's whisper had her jumping. "Then again, rumor has it he's got more tattoos than the uniform lets on and some fun piercings to go with them."

"Don't we all?" Gwen ignored the calls from her friend as she stole a page from Jensen's book and walked away. A girl needs to have a few surprises up her sleeve.

She stepped out of the station, took a deep breath of the cold, late winter air and brushed the snow off the top of the picnic table before taking a seat. She leaned back against the building and the rough brick bit into her back the slightest bit as she allowed her eyes to drift shut.

"I'm sure there are plenty of beds in the station if you need a nap that badly."

She looked at the petite woman who stood across from her. "There are, but there are also a lot of people in there. People equal noise." She sat up straight. "How did you get back here?"

The stranger looked around the fenced in area, her green eyes sparkling as the light reflected off the snow. "I'm not really sure. I was supposed to meet with Chief Keetes about ten minutes ago, but there was no one at the front desk when I came in, so I wandered around and you were the first person I found."

"It's Saturday. Our secretary has the day off, and God only knows where the chief is." She felt the jealousy flair for a second before she was able to tamp it down. Hell, he had hardly spoken to her before a couple of months ago. She had no claim.

"I am the new guy, er, girl, I guess. I start next shift, but the chief wanted me to come in today so he could introduce me and finish the paper work."

Gwen shook the woman's hand. "We can always use another girl around here. I'm Gwen, one of the medics on this shift."

"Nice to meet you. The other medic is a woman, too, right?" At Gwen's nod, she chattered on. "I thought so. I saw her on the news when that building collapsed on the old chief and her—"

Gwen felt a sharp pain in her chest as the world around her faded. Her palms grew clammy and the memories flooded her system.

She pushed the drugs, giving Leland some relief from the pain just as the rear doors of the rig swung open. Three soot covered firemen struggled to hold onto Kevin's limp form. His bunker gear stained red. His eyes fixed. Motionless.

"Gwen? Gwendolyn! Look at me." Hands wrapped around her upper arms and gave her a shake, pulling her from her memory. "Gwendolyn, look at me!"

She felt the cold breeze on her sweat covered face. "I'm looking at you, Jensen."

"No, you are looking *through* me. Focus your eyes and look *at* me." The command in his voice managed to pull her securely into the present. "That's my girl. Stop scowling at me."

Her scowl deepened. "You can't praise me in one breath and scold me in the next."

He released her arms and smiled. "The hell I can't. It is literally in my job description."

She rolled her eyes. "You need a dictionary. There is no way that is *literally* in your job description."

"Oh the sass. She's fine."

"I'm sorry, Gwen. I didn't mean to—" the woman started, only to be cut off by the concerned man next to her.

"What happened? Don't turn away from me."

"I'm fine, Jensen."

"As your boss, at the very least, you owe me an explanation, but as your friend, I need to know you are okay."

She turned her narrowed eyes on the man. "You fight dirty."

"No, I simply use every advantage I have. It just so happens one of those advantages is that you're madly in love with me."

Gwen groaned, "I have never said or even hinted that I'm madly in love with you."

"Oh, the hints are there, baby. As far as the words go, I will be hearing them soon enough."

Before Gwen could retort, a throat was cleared. "I'm sorry, but this looks like it is about to get all hot and heavy, and I am pretty sure the two of you forgot I was standing here."

Heat crept into Gwen's face, but she held the eyes of the cocky man in front of her. "Way to go, *Chief*. You embarrassed the new girl!"

"Embarrassed her?" He scuffed. "If she is going to be working here, she should probably get used to being embarrassed. Especially with this shift."

"Am I missing something?"

"There is no reason for this to be so hard. He wants you, you want him. Quit pussyfooting around it and go for it already." The exasperation was evident in Autumn's voice. "The conversation the two of you had this morning should have been enough to crush any remaining doubt."

"Why can't he just snatch me away and make me his?"

"The same reason Autumn enlisted you in her plot to get me to ask her to move in." At the confused expressions, Leland continued. "We can't read your minds. Not to mention, kidnapping charges would not look good on the new fire chief's record."

"Nah." The women waved him off.

"Look, he may be the Dom, but you hold all the power.

Which means, if you want this, you have to make a move."

"Oh, quit giving him that look. He's telling you the truth. It only looks like the Dom has all the control, but we subs are a pretty powerful bunch."

"Prove it."

Autumn pondered for a second before she snapped her fingers. "It's like a coloring book and crayons. Submissives are the coloring books. They lay out all the lines and boundaries. Dominants are the crayons. They can color that page any way they want as long as they stay within the lines set by the sub."

"We mostly use red. We *really* like red."

"I swear. I am trying to help a girl out here, and all you can think about is slapping my ass."

Jensen cleared his throat from behind them. "If you three hens are done clucking, I would like to start the meeting."

His whisper ended with a grunt when Leland's fist met his gut. "I'll show you a hen."

Jensen chuckled as he walked to the front of the room. "We have a couple of things that need to be addressed." He nodded, and the new girl joined him. "This is Kennly Foller. She will be starting next shift. I know you all will make her feel at home on C-shift." He nodded again, and she took a seat next to Gwen. "As some of you have assumed, the arsonist had made contact with the fire marshal."

"And here I was just getting used to sleeping at night again."

"That's just it; this letter was a little different. It only mentioned that he would be in touch. None of his usual compliments, criticisms, or niceties. And it didn't arrive to the marshal when it usually does, so I am putting us on alert. Be prepared. Now, I am going to let the detectives have the floor."

Gwen watched as three men made their way into the room. Whispered conversations tittered around them, until Davis' voice rose above the quiet drone. "They think the arsonist is one of us!"

"You think we killed one of our own!"

"Are you fucking kidding me?"

"Enough!" Jensen shot daggers at each man who tried to argue with him. "PD is here because they suspect someone is using our IP address illegally. Nothing more."

"Bullshit. If that was all they thought this was, they would have sent someone over from IT to update our security and passwords. There is more to it than some teen stealing our internet."

"You're right." Detective Starling held up his hand, silencing Jensen. "There is more to this, but we aren't sure what. So, while we work all this out, we are all stuck working together. I don't like it any more than the rest of you. If it *is* the arsonist, we need to be ready."

"Can't your geeks do this remotely, Starling? The last thing we need is this guy figuring out that we are on to him." Zander paced the back of the room as he ran his hand over his hair.

"Gee, why didn't I think of that?"

"Okay, I was just—"

"Just what? Trying to do my job for me?" Starling's knuckles popped as he fisted his hands at his side. His swift change from placating to on the defensive was unsettling. "You think I want to spend my days in this hell hole? I would much rather be at my desk back at the station. At least that place doesn't smell like sweaty men and smoke."

"More like doughnuts and crispy bacon."

"Who said that? You assholes think this is funny? I am working my ass off to solve this case, and all you fuckers can do is make jokes?"

"Calm down, Star—"

"Fuck you, Keetes. I have other cases that need my attention, but here I am, slumming with the help. For what?" Startling threw a hand out in Zander's direction. "So this fucker can question how I do my job?"

"I wasn't questioning you. I simply *had* a question."

In an instant, Starling stalked to the back of the room and

was nose to nose with Zander. "There's no difference."

Zander held his hands in the air, placating. "Man, I was just asking."

"Don't 'man' me after that insult. You think you could do a better job, be my guest."

"All. I did. Was ask."

Anger rolled off the two men. In an instant, Starling shoved Zander, forcing him to take a couple of steps back. Just as Starling went to take a step forward, Kennly wedged herself between the two men, her back to Zander's chest. "Enough."

"Fuck you." Starling grabbed her roughly by the forearm. Without much effort, she broke the hold. As soon as she did, Zander physically picked the woman up and placed her behind him, out of harm's way.

"Holy shit," Gwen whispered as she watched one of the other officers wrench Starling's hand behind his back, forcing him to the ground. With his potbelly to the floor, he quickly gave up the fight and just lay there panting between words. "I will have your job for this, Bass." He nodded to Zander. "And yours."

"Try it. I didn't lay a hand on you, and neither did she. We will be filing a complaint with HR." When Starling lunged again, the other officers were barely able to hold him back. "Get out of our station before you give us more ammunition in our quest for *your* badge."

"Back off, Starling," one of the other officers commanded as he joined the crowd and helped pull the man to his feet.

As soon as the door closed behind the infuriated man, another officer stepped forward, his slight accent thickening with anger. "I'm Officer Thomas. Oisin Thomas. On behalf of all my brothers in blue, I'm sorry for that. Not all of us are as hot headed as he is."

"Seems you're constantly making apologies for Detective Starling," Autumn deadpanned.

"Feels that way, too. As for your question, Zander, we tried.

Our IT guys have been working on it for a few days now, but the firewall is too good. None of our 'geeks' have been able to get through it. We are hoping that if we come at it from a different angle, we will find a weak point and be able to put a hole in his defenses."

"Tell them the rest," Jensen commanded. "If you want them to cooperate, even help, you have to tell them."

"We have reason to believe that Miss Boisy is being monitored."

"Wait. My sister is connected to this?" Leland's fist clenched in his lap.

"Her name kept popping up. When we could no longer pretend it was coincidence, we got her permission to look at her computer." With a sigh, he continued. "We found that two different IP addresses had been used to remotely access her computer. We were able to trace one of them back here."

"And the other?" Zander's voice was little more than a growl.

"It has been pinged around the world so many times, we haven't been able to track it down yet, but we will."

"Seems to me that is the one you should be focused on," one of the men protested.

"And if it were your sister in the crosshairs of an arsonist turned murderer, would you be satisfied with them only following up on one lead?" When he was met with only silence, Leland continued. "I didn't think so. Do your job; you have our total support."

With that, the cops dispersed, and Jensen walked to the front of the room. "I expect everyone to cooperate with them. They are here to do their jobs, just like us."

As the meeting ended, Gwen sought out Kennly. "It is nice to have a name to go with the woman."

Before Kennly could respond, a determined Zander took hold of her wrist and pulled her from the room. "Excuse us, Gwen, I need to show *Kennly* around the station." The whispered conversation between the two of them faded fast as they rounded the corner.

"That looked interesting," Autumn stage whispered.

"Yeah, something is going on there. I'd put money on that."

"Speaking of bets, you have to tell me what you have pierced. I bet Leland I could get you to tell me."

"Not a chance."

"If I bribe you with wine and pizza, will you spill?"

She paused in her retreat and turned back to her friend. "Girls only and you pay?"

"Just the two of us, or can we invite Sierra and Liv?" Autumn questioned.

"It wouldn't really be a girls' night out without them. Oh, and invite the new girl." Autumn did a premature victory dance. "This doesn't mean you're getting those secrets out of me, but free food and drinks is a big step in the right direction."

"Good. The night after next?"

"Tomorrow night would work better."

"Sorry. You already have plans with the chief for supper."

Gwen watched as her friend practically ran from the room.

"You can't truly be surprised she stuck her nose where it didn't belong." Leland smiled as he watched his girl skirt around a corner and disappear.

"I know. Truthfully, I think that was why I was complaining to her about it. I knew she would eventually take the choice out of my hands." She turned to the man beside her. "Can you at least fill me in on the details?"

"All I know is that you are supposed to be ready to go tomorrow night at seven. Oh, and the girls will be there to help you get ready at five."

"Five? Who needs two hours to get ready for a date?" She watched him walk away without even attempting to answer her question. "And why does everyone keep walking away from me when I'm talking to them?"

Chapter 2

It turned out that she didn't need two hours to get ready for her date. The ladies who invaded her house needed two hours to gossip, drink wine and pick out her outfit.

"I am telling you, she needs to wear the red dress with those cute strappy heels." Liv fell back on the bed before she kicked her own shoes off.

"It's thirty degrees outside. If she goes out in those shoes, she is going to lose a few toes."

Sierra's voice was muffled from inside the closet. "Oh, look at this!" Her arm appeared around one of the sliding doors.

"No, that's too cute, we're going for sexy."

When the doorbell sounded, everyone, except Gwen, frantically searched for the time. "He's early!"

"By about three minutes," Gwen laughed as she grabbed her purse off the back of the chair.

"But we still don't know what you're going to wear!"

"I have known what I was going to wear since this morning." She smiled at her friends before she looked down at her red sweater dress that ended just above her knee.

"What about shoes?"

"My black boots look amazing with this outfit."

Autumn looked her up and down. "I guess that will work."

Gwen snorted a laugh as she walked out of the room. At the door, she smoothed her dress down before swinging it open. "Did you check the peep hole before opening the door?" She looked guiltily to the floor as hope blossomed in her belly. "That is answer enough. First rule of the night, always check before you open the door. Deal?"

She smiled as she picked up her boots. "I can handle that."

"You're early." The accusation was followed by a grunt as one of the girls, no doubt, elbowed Sierra for giving up their location.

"Do I need to come back in?" He looked at his watch. "Thirty seconds?"

"And leave me here with them? Not a chance."

"I am *so* glad we picked that outfit for her. She looks hot." The laughter from the hall had Gwen rolling her eyes.

"Where are we going?" Gwen questioned as she put her arms into the coat he was holding out for her.

"I thought we could try out the new Mexican joint on Frank Ave."

"I heard their salsa is to die for."

Jensen held the door open for her to precede him before calling back, "Good night, ladies."

"I have to have more chips," Gwen said as she waved down the waiter. "What? Do I have something in my teeth?"

"No, I just…I love that you skipped dessert for chips."

"Freshly made chips *and* salsa."

"Of course."

"Don't get me wrong; I love dessert just like the next girl, but," she looked around before leaning toward him. "This is free." She watched him toss his head back and laugh as she grabbed a hot chip from the basket.

"I like this."

"I am going to guess you aren't talking about the chips."

"Smart ass. No, I'm talking about seeing you some place other than the station. You, in something other than your uniform, watching you light up over something as simple as free chips."

"I like it, too." She shoved a salsa-laden chip in her mouth and spoke around it. "So, what does that mean?"

"It means we do this again."

"I would like that." She picked at the wicker basket. It seemed like she was always looking for ways to avoid eye contact with the man. "So, that means?"

When she didn't continue, he tipped her face up so he could catch her eyes. "That you're mine."

"And you're mine?"

"Cheeky, girl. Yes, but if you think you get the same perks I do, you're sorely mistaken. That smirk of yours is going to get you in so much trouble."

His comment only made her smile grow. "What perks are we talking about here? I scratch your back, you scratch mine?"

"More like I paddle your ass, you get subspace. If you're a good girl." He watched her closely for a while. "Gwen, take a breath before you pass out."

She did as he suggested, dragging some much-needed oxygen into her lungs. "And if I'm a bad girl?"

"Those perks are all mine."

She pulled her chin out of his grasp and picked up another chip. "So, I just check the peep hole and we are right as rain?"

"Not quite. Do you know the four D's?"

"No disrespect, dishonor, disobedience and… I can never remember the last one."

"The most important of all of them." He shook his head in

mock disappointment. "No danger. Can you abide by those rules?"

"I'm not sure how I would dishonor you, but I think I handle those rules as long as you don't expect me to be spineless or give up my, at times, dangerous job."

"I would never intervene with your career as your Dom, but as your boss, that may be another story."

"You think it can work? Like you said, you're my boss."

"I wouldn't be here if I didn't, but you need to know that I will not hide our relationship from anyone at the station. They need to know."

She chewed her lip. "Not even for a little bit?"

"Nope."

"Why?"

"Frankly, so they can pick up the slack when I am distracted by you. Like you said, we have dangerous jobs, and I will undoubtedly worry about you. I already do. With the others knowing we are together, they can anticipate that I may need a little help keeping my head in the game or keeping track of you."

"Okay, what about while we are at work?" When he opened his mouth, she hurried on. "Hold on. I don't expect you to turn off the Dom, I know that isn't how it works, but I would like to limit the amount of Dom you get to exert on me while at work."

"Are you telling me that you don't want to frequent the supply closet as your cohort does?"

"No, I am saying I don't want you demanding me to kneel at your feet at the station when I piss you off."

His hand disappeared under the table as he grunted. "Warn a guy when you are going to paint such a pretty picture." He nodded at the next table before he continued on in a whisper, "I think she got an eye full of me trying to discreetly adjust my cock." Water went everywhere as Gwen coughed into her glass. "You okay?"

"Turnabout is fair play." Gwen wheezed as she mopped her

face and the table with a wad of napkins. "Think we have embarrassed ourselves here enough?"

"Absolutely, but I have one more place I need to go before I take you home. It's on the way."

"Should I be nervous?

"Only if you're opposed to the cold."

"I cannot believe we are trespassing on someone's property," Gwen whispered as they rounded the side of a beautiful ranch style house.

"Why are you whispering?"

"Because you asked me if I was good with being cold, not if I was okay with criminal charges. Quit laughing at me. I don't find this funny."

Jensen laughed as he mounted the stairs to the deck. "Gwen, we pulled into the driveway, right up to the garage. Do you really think we are trespassing?"

She paused for a second. "Why didn't we go to the door and knock?"

"Two reasons. First, no one is home. I am here to let George out. Second, if they were home and I knocked on the door at this time of night, my dad would be pissed and then my ma would read me the riot act for knocking rather than just walking in."

"This is your parents' house? Wait, who is George?"

Jensen went to the patio door and slid it open. "Gwen, meet George. He is my mom's baby. I'm pretty sure she treats him better than she does me."

Gwen sat on the cold wood of the deck. "Oh my gosh! He is so cute!" As she scratched the dog behind his perked ears, she turned to Jensen. "He doesn't look like a George."

He chuckled. "My dad made it clear that if he was going to

be stuck with this ball of fluff for the next ten years, he was not going to be stuck calling it some stupid name."

"George isn't stupid."

"Not according to Greg Keetes. Take him to the yard, baby; he won't go out there without someone with him. I'll be right back."

Gwen managed to keep from melting into a puddle when he used the pet name, but just so. "Come on, George." As she walked in the snow, she thought about their night. She couldn't remember the last time she had laughed as much as she had, let alone felt this relaxed with a man. "I could get used to dates like these," she told the pup as he ran circles around her, kicking up snow as he went. "Come on; I have an idea."

Chapter 3

"Gwen, do you like—" That was all the further he got before a cold splat hit him in the chest. "Where are you, brat?" He laughed as the dog gave up her position. "Good boy, George."

"Traitor," Gwen accused from the side of the deck.

"Give it up, Gwendolyn. I have not lost a snowball fight in all my thirty-five years."

"There's a first time for everything. Even if I do lose, I have enough ammo down here to put up a good fight. Come get me."

"Challenge accepted." He set the mugs on the railing before he scooped up a handful of the fluffy snow. He didn't even get to the bottom of the steps before a snowball whizzed past his head. "You have to hit me in order to win."

"Eh, that was just one miss; I have plenty more." The next one hit him in the side of the head. "Bullseye!" She ran around the side of the house, George barking as he chased after her.

Jensen smiled as he meandered in the same direction, the joy growing in his chest. Another clump of snow hit him in the leg, trailed by another miss. He ducked behind a tree, just managing to side step another of her projectiles. He blindly tossed his own back at her. "You are going to use up all your ammunition."

"You were in the house a long time. George and I have plenty to defend ourselves."

"I have a couple of advantages over you."

"Do share."

He smiled at the laughter in her voice.

A snowball sailed past him. That was his cue. He stepped from behind the tree and dashed to the next one. "I was in the house for a while. I'm warm. My guess is that the cold is starting to seep through your coat and gloves right about now." The lull in the snowballs attacking the defenseless tree he had been hiding behind was answer enough. "That's what I thought."

"I'll survive." As soon as the snowballs started to fly again, he moved, ducking behind trees as he went, keeping to the shadows and staying low. "And your other advantages?" He looked at the impressive, but dwindling, pile of snowballs next to her. "Jensen?"

"I know the terrain," he whispered into her ear from behind, causing her to startle, right before he grabbed her around the waist and lifted her off her feet.

"No! I was supposed to win!"

"Sometimes things don't go as they are supposed to."

"Wait! I'm wearing a dress!" she squealed as he laid her in the snow and settled on top of her.

"Your coat is long enough; one kiss in the snow won't hurt anything." He captured the rest of her protests with his mouth. He intended for it to be a quick kiss. With the snow at her back, it had to be quick, but when she boldly wrapped her legs around his waist, all thoughts of the cold vanished.

He gave her more of his weight as he ran a hand from where her boot ended on her calf up her leg as far as her tightly buttoned coat would allow. With hooded eyes, he watched her pull off her gloves before she shoved her cold hands under his coat and into his shirt, wrapping them around his back, wordlessly asking for more.

He nipped at her chin sharply. When she gasped from the quick bite of pain, he dove in for another kiss, taking all she was willing to give. When she pulled away, gasping for breath, he trailed the kiss along her jaw and down her throat.

"Jensen." The single, groaned word had him grinding his hard cock into her soft belly. The resulting moan from the woman under him had him reaching for his zipper with one hand and the buttons of her coat with the other.

It was the sharp bark that stopped him, pulling him from his need long enough to remind him where they were. Reluctantly, he stood, bringing her with him. "Sorry, bellissima, I got carried away."

"But."

Her pout was adorable. "Not like this. And before any of those lies take root in your head, I want you. Far too much." He guided her hand to his bulging zipper. "But if we keep going, one of us is going to get frostbite." He led her to the deck. "Let's put George back in the house and then we can warm up with some cocoa."

"I have some bad news." Gwen turned to him, holding the discarded mugs. "The hot chocolate isn't very hot anymore."

Chapter 4

"How big was it?"

"You heard me right."

Gwen snorted a laugh as her head fell to the table. She could feel her face heat as the wine took effect and laughter took over.

They had been at the sports bar for a few hours and were just getting to the good stuff. She lifted her head from the table and pushed her curls from her face.

"And you let him put it in your ass!" The girls looked at Kennly like she was dense. "What? I've never had anything in my butt."

"It is deliciously awful, but mostly delicious. I always have my safeword, but trust me, octopus was the last thing I was thinking of." Autumn visibly shivered. "Plugs are well within the lines of my coloring book." Laughter erupted around the table. "However, I'm starting to think I should reconsider denial being within those lines."

"You brought that on yourself."

"Liv! You're supposed to be on my side!"

"I am, but everyone knows that when you are offered an

orgasm, you take it." She pushed her purple tipped hair out of her face.

Autumn snorted. "I wasn't offered one. I was ordered to beg for one."

Gwen raked her fingers through her hair, throwing the mass of curls everywhere. "I still can't believe you refused an offered orgasm? Are you mad?"

"No." Liv smiled at her friend. "She's just stubborn. You can wipe that fake look of shock off your face, Autumn Rose. You've forgotten how well I know you. He *wanted* you to beg, and you refused just for the sake of being stubborn. When I did that with Kevin, he used to make me wait even longer for the next one. The last time I failed to 'beg prettily', as he called it, he refused me pleasure for a week. I hope your Dom has more mercy than mine did."

"I doubt it." She chewed her lip as she wiggled in her seat. "He literally wanted me on my knees begging for more. I went to my knees, but the words just wouldn't come." Gwen watched as Liv and Sierra both cringed. "Right? We were just having fun, so I am not in any real trouble, but he did take offence to his sub refusing his demand. Long story short, he bent me over the couch and put an even bigger plug in my ass and told me I was to wear it until he personally took it out."

Gwen snorted. "Was that before or after he gave you the drink limit that you just passed." She watched as realization hit her friend between the eyes. With a smirk, she turned to the other women at the table, "Now she is trying to remember if he told her what implement he would use if she went over her limit."

"Keep laughing, you three; it's only a matter of time before you have Doms and it's you guys thinking this exact same thing."

"Mine didn't give me a limit tonight." All eyes swung to Sierra. "What?"

"You're seeing someone?" Gwen caught the secret smile on Autumn's face. "You knew about this?"

"I just knew she had met someone. I didn't know they were dating."

"We aren't dating, at this point, but we have played together a couple of times."

"Safely?"

"At monitored clubs, yes." The women looked at each other for a few seconds before the cheers erupted around the table. "Okay, okay, enough. I want to hear about the surprises Gwen will be revealing to the chief when she finally jumps his bones."

"No."

"Yes."

Gwen narrowed her eyes at the women across from her. "There is nothing to tell. Autumn just has an overactive imagination."

"You know this shift has no secrets from each other. Hell, I have seen Kennly naked at the club more times than I can count. I have yet to figure out who she keeps sneaking away with. Ouch. Why is everyone kicking me?"

"Maybe because you have a big mouth. Maybe because Kennly didn't want everyone here to know that she was into the kinky stuff."

"Thank you, Liv, but that's not why I kicked her. Hell, I have seen everyone at the club except Gwen. That was part of the reason I was so excited to find out I was going to be on C-shift. What I don't want is everyone thinking is that who I play with is a big secret. I mean, we don't want everyone knowing yet, but it isn't a secret." She paused, allowing her eyes to shift to Sierra for a second before they fell to her lap. "That made more sense in my head."

"Gwen's 'new' to this scene," Sierra so helpfully pointed out as she took a sip of her pink drink.

"I'm not new; I'm rusty."

"Rusty? What are you, the tinman?" Autumn winked as the smile grew on her face.

"Oh, I hate those flying monkeys." Sierra visibly shivered.

"I was thinking she was more like the scarecrow, as in needing a brain, because she would have to be crazy to put off hooking up with Jensen." Kennly's eyes rolled back in her head as she moaned her appreciation.

"Hey, I was all for a romp in the snow. He was the one who decided he didn't want to get frostbite."

"Oh!" Sierra bounced in her seat. "She's totally the lion. Anyone attempting to take on that bossy, hunk of a man has to be courageous."

"No," Liv said from her seat, her eyes soft and knowing. "For this to be any good for her, she must be willing to give up her heart. Handing over her damaged one scares the crap out of her." She reached across the table and squeezed Gwen's hand. "There is no question in my mind that she is the tinman looking for a heart.

"Fuck. Waiter, another round! This shit is getting heavy. Oh, but make mine a diet Coke."

"Autumn!" Sierra shook her head disapprovingly. "I swear to God, the bar across the street heard you yell. Hasn't my brother put a stop to your swearing yet?"

"He isn't here; I'm safe."

The table erupted in laughter. "You really believe that?"

"Of course, I do." She hesitated for a second. "Well, safe for now."

Sierra huffed. "If you think so."

Kennly snorted. "At least you're not the only one lying to yourself. Gwen, over here, still thinks we aren't going to know what treasures she is hiding from us by the end of the night."

"There are no treasures."

"Liar!" Autumn's fist bounced off the table.

"Give us a little hint."

"Yeah, please. You know we won't let up until you do."

Gwen looked around the table; all of the girls were throwing their best pleading look in her direction. "Fine. I just have a couple of tattoos and one or two strategically placed piercings."

"Piercings? As in more than one?"

"Maybe." She shrugged. "Maybe I just lied, and I don't have any."

The flat of Liv's hand hit the table hard. "All this time, I thought you were the innocent one out of all of us. You have been holding back, Gwendolyn. Spill."

"Not a chance."

"There are ways to make you talk." The faint crinkling at the corner of her eyes was the only outward hint that Kennly was joking.

"I have been tortured by the best of them, but you are more than welcome to try."

"I'm not talking torture. I'm talking interrogation. You would be surprised how much simply answering a few questions can give away. I bet I could crack you in four questions."

"Someone was a cop in a past life."

"Nope. My dad was an officer for thirty-two years, taught me everything I know."

Liv snorted. "Decided to give your dad someone to look up to and become a firefighter, huh?"

"That is exactly what he said when I told him what I was going into."

"It doesn't matter. I am keeping this, or these, secrets for myself."

"Please," Sierra pled, her hands folded in front of her.

"Sorry. The surprised look on his face when you remove your clothes and the light reflects off the sparkling barbell…" Gwen's eye closed as a moan slipped from her lips. "…you only get that if they don't already know about the surprises. I know one of you will blow that for me if given the chance, so I hold my cards close to my chest."

"I don't know if I should be mad at you for not telling us or proud of you." The look on Autumn's face mirrored that of a proud mother.

"You guys do know that the piercing you are all so proud of could just be my belly button, right?"

The four women looked back and forth between each other before they all spoke at the same time. "No."

"So, who is going to tell me what he's got?" The women shrugged. "Come on! He is one of the Doms you guys party with. You must have seen it. Them? Whatever, you have to have seen it."

"I've never seen him play. Haven't been to enough parties yet," Autumn said before she turned to the other girls.

Sierra held up her hands. "Don't look at me! I am out of there before it gets too hot and heavy. Last thing I want to see is my brother doing his thing. Gross."

"Liv?"

There was no denying the guilt on Liv's face. "Yes?"

"You've seen them! Spill," Autumn demanded as she waved down a waiter.

"I have not."

"Shit, I hope you don't play poker with that tell." Kennly took a pull from her beer.

"Fine, I have seen, but I can't tell you."

"I'll beg," Autumn offered with a smirk on her face.

"No."

Autumn's smiled widened as she stood from the booth. "Last chance, Liv. Spill, or I start begging."

Liv narrowed her eyes. "You wouldn't beg your man for an orgasm, but you're going to beg me in a room full of people?" Liv had barely gotten the words out before Autumn fell to her knees in the middle of the bar, her hands clasped as if she was praying. "Don't. You. Dare."

Autumn waited, giving Liv another chance, before she started speaking loudly. "Please, Mistress Liv! Please bestow on us the vast knowledge you have gained over the years."

"This is the reason Leland limits the number of drinks you're allowed." Gwen sank deeper into the chair.

"I can't tell you."

Autumn ignored the comments as well as the tittering that had started around the room and continued. "Why must you keep the secrets locked within you, Mistress Liv? All I ask is for you to share your wisdom."

"I need a fucking safeword," Liv cursed.

A nervous waitress tapped Autumn on the shoulder. "Miss, I am going to have to ask you to get off the floor. You're blocking the path to the exit, and it's against fire code."

Gwen snorted. "And your Dom is a firefighter!" Laughter erupted around the table.

Back in the booth, Autumn leaned into Liv. "Pretty please, Liv-a-luscious."

"Look, I can't tell any of you. I wouldn't be allowed to another party, and let's face it, I need those parties."

Everyone at the table instantly became serious. "You've been to parties since he died? Have you participated?"

"God, no! I just… I just go to watch the people. Like we used to do."

"Does it help?" Gwen grasped Liv's hand.

"I think so. Being around the people he loved makes me feel closer to him, and I need that so *fucking* bad right now." Liv picked at her nails for a few seconds before she gave herself a little shake. "I'm sorry, but I am not willing to risk that so you guys can be in on a little secret. Come to the parties and find out for yourselves."

"Or we can keep guessing and see what we come up with."

Kennly smiled evilly. "By the end of the night, their actual secrets are going to look like child's play compared to what we come up with."

"What has the four of you laughing so hard?" Jensen questioned as he and Leland sauntered up to the booth a couple hours later.

"I swear to God, Jensen, if you have a Prince Albert piercing, there is going to be a line of women wanting to try it."

"Sierra!"

"Don't worry, brother, I didn't say I was going to be in that line." She turned to the woman beside her, her whisper not nearly as quiet as she intended for it to be, "I'm totally going to be in that line."

"Where's Kennly?"

"She went home a couple hours ago, and the laughter started out as wine giggles, but now it is probably a result of the tequila," Autumn shared as Jensen sat on the edge of the booth, forcing Gwen to give him room.

"Forget the giggles; that's all these women do when they're together. I want to hear more about the pretty dark-haired woman who begged so prettily in front of a room full of people," Leland growled as he, too, took a seat on the end of the booth, forcing Autumn to move over, and sank his hand in her dark strands.

"Who told?"

Before Autumn could stare down the other women, Leland's fist closed in her hair and her chin was caught in his free hand. "No one told, princess. It was all the men sitting at the bar could talk about when we walked in."

"That, and something about the bastard lucky enough to claim her."

Gwen elbowed the man sitting next to her. "You're not helping her any."

"I know. All I heard this fool talk about all night was how she refused to do as she was told, so I figure I'm due for some pay back."

"Uh-oh," Gwen loudly whispered to Liv and Sierra. "Did you see that look cross his face? I can't tell if she's in trouble, or if he is turned on."

"Both," Liv concluded as she stuck her hand into her glass in pursuit of an olive. With a smile, she popped it into her mouth as she looked around the room. "I need more beer-soaked olives."

"No, you don't. I think you've all had plenty. Autumn?"

"Just pop for the last few hours, but I did go one drink over my limit, Sir."

He pulled on a lock of her hair. "Princess."

Laying her head on the back of the booth, Gwen sighed. "He smells really good, you guys." Jensen looked down at her, and her liquor-laden brain focused solely on his lips. "If I were to kiss you right now, would you make me stop before we go too hot and heavy in the snow?"

A big smile split his face. "How much have you had to drink?"

She curled her lips. "Not so many that I had to break out my credit card, but then again, Autumn was buying, so it is anyone's guess. You didn't give me a limit, right? We tried to pry your secrets out of Liv, but she wouldn't give them up."

He laughed softly. "You're very honest when you're drunk. And, no, there was no limit, but it looks like there should have been."

"I'm always honest. The alcohol just has my thought to mouth filter on the fritz." She rubbed his bald head. "Bald looks good on you. It makes your goatee look thicker, and the bad boy look works for you. Especially when you are in your bunker gear."

"Right!" Autumn agreed. "I keep trying to talk Leland into bringing his gear home so we can play with it, but he says 'no'."

"Quit pouting at me, princess. I have told you a million times, my gear is too dirty to play in."

"But it would be *so* much fun!"

"Kevin and I did it once." When both the guys turned their glares on her, Liv only shrugged. "It was when you guys got new gear. He brought home a set before you swapped them out for the old sets. It was hot as fuck. The Velcro fly scratched the shit out of his cock when I was giving him a blow job, but he didn't complain until the next morning."

"See?" Gwen whined as she nudged Jensen. "Hot. Oh, and do one of those sexy, almost, but not quite, pornographic photo shoots in them."

Autumn snapped her fingers. "You mean a boudoir shoot!"

"Yes."

"Moan like that again, and I will not be responsible for my actions."

Gwen opened one of her eyes as a smirk played on her lips. "Promises, promises."

"I think you may have your hands full, Key." Leland laughed as he stood and hauled his girlfriend to her feet. "Come on, you three; let's get you home. You got her, Keetes?"

"Yeah. Come on, it's time for bed."

"Okay, but I will get a hold of your gear one way or another." She grabbed her purse and shoved her hair out of her face for the millionth time that night. "One of these days, I'm going to take a pair of scissors to this mess."

"You cut off that gorgeous hair, and I will beat your ass." His lips curled into a devilish grin. "I felt that shiver."

"I know. It was such a good shiver, too."

Chapter 5

He held her hair as she retched into the toilet. "My palm is itching."

"You should probably get that checked out."

"That would have been much funnier if it hadn't just echoed off the toilet bowl you currently have your head in." A moan was her only response. "God, you are so lucky you're sick."

"Need to find relief for that itchy palm?"

"My palm will have to wait to meet your ass until morning." She scowled at him as she rested her head on the toilet seat. "Don't look at me like that. I would never punish while you are ill."

"Sick equals free rein. Got it."

He laughed. "No, it means I save it for when you are better. That way, I know you will remember it."

"And not puke all over you." She sighed. "I'm only twenty-four hours into this thing, and I've already messed up."

"You're human; it was bound to happen at some point." He leaned closer to her. "But if you roll your eyes at me like that again, bellissima, I may forget how sick you are."

He watched as her face softened. "What did you call me?"

"Bellissima, it's Italian for beautiful. It suits you. Do you like it?" The only response he got was a lazy smile that tugged on the corners of her mouth. "Good. Now, my next question is very important. We just started this relationship, and I didn't tell you that you had a drink limit, so you have a choice to make. If I leave tonight, I will not spank you, but if I stay, your ass will feel my hand in the morning. You choose how you want to proceed." In a second, the compliant look on her face was gone and the spitfire he had grown to know and appreciate was back. *She'll make me earn her submission every time.*

"You may not have noticed, but every girl in that station, on our shift or otherwise, has been volleying for a chance for you to notice her. Me, I have always stood quietly in the back. I'm done with that. I did it for *way* too long." Swallowing hard, she continued. "At his funeral, I promised Kevin I wouldn't waste my gift of life in the back of the crowd. It's time I start fulfilling that promise." She snorted. "Until this last shift, I was clueless that you had any interest in me. I thought you found me atrocious, truthfully."

His eyes narrowed as he pinched her thigh right where the skirt of her dress ended. With a growl, he brought his lips to her ear. "The only reason you are not wearing my handprint on your thigh is because I didn't want you to start puking again. You are never to talk about my girl that way again. Do you understand me, bellissima?" At her nod, he leaned back, so she could see his face once more, and smiled. "Consider that your one and only warning."

"And here I am with my head in the toilet on this momentous occasion."

Jensen chuckled. "You weren't lying when you said your filters don't work when you drink. Am I going to have to worry about you every time you go out with the girls?"

"I'm going to say no, but you'll worry anyway. You Doms are always looking for more reasons to beat our asses."

"Spank. Never beat. And I have my ways of making sure you remember our rules even when you don't particularly want to." He rubbed his hand soothingly up and down her back. "Are you ready for me to get you into bed yet?"

Her pout nearly had him laughing. "You're going to make me sleep there all by myself, aren't you?"

"No, that is all up to you, but if you choose to have me stay, sleeping is all we will be doing tonight. Either way, I will stay with you until I'm sure you aren't going to vomit all over yourself. Now, let's go before any more of your hair falls into the toilet."

She gasped when he scooped her into his arms. "Why the long sleeves all the time?"

"Not all the time. Which room?"

"The door at the end of the hall. That's all I've ever seen you in."

"That's because that's what I wear to work, and besides last night and now, we have not seen each other anywhere but work." He sat her on the bed and looked down at her, waiting for what he knew was coming.

"You weren't at work tonight, and it's March; it's practically boiling outside."

He rolled his eyes. "Forty degrees is not boiling, especially when you're used to being in bunker gear and fight fires for a living. Now, we get you into bed. I'll get you some clean clothes."

"I can sleep in these."

He shook his head as she slightly swayed, taking a second to make sure she wasn't going to fall off the bed, before he turned to the dresser. "What do you wear to bed?"

"A tee. Bottom drawer," Gwen said through a yawn.

"That's all you wear?" He groaned as he grabbed a shirt. "This image is going to cause me many hard, sleepless nights to come."

He turned back to the bed expecting a smart, drunken come

back, but all he got was silence from the woman now sprawled across the foot of the bed. "Shit."

Her auburn hair was feathered across the quilt, her mouth agape. He tried hard not to let his eyes stray from her face, but her skirt had ridden up her thighs and the newly exposed creamy flesh called to him. He crudely adjusted his cock within the confines of his jeans. With a deep breath, he went to work carefully removing her boots and socks before taking a seat on the bed. He glanced up the length of her body, and her eyes cracked open.

"I can do the rest."

He laughed. "Were you faking, Gwendolyn?"

"I puked in front of a really hot guy. That tends to sober a girl up real quick."

"It also makes you flush a hundred shades of red."

She sat up and grabbed the tee from his hands. In a second, her dress was over her head and she was covered in only a black, lace pair of boy shorts and a nude colored bra. "Here I thought girls made sure to match their underwear with their bra."

She snorted as she pulled the shirt over her head, not allowing him to get a better look. "Lies! All lies."

"Was that a tattoo?"

She shrugged. "You don't get to see that yet."

"Okay, do you have any matching bras and panties?"

"Of course, I do, but I don't ever match them, too much work. Unless I am planning on getting laid."

"Good to know. So, why torture an innocent man?" At her puzzled expression, he continued. "Your dress rode up on your thighs." She absently twirled her hair between her fingers, her eyes still closed. He grasped her hand and gently pulled it from her hair. "Oh, no. You don't get to go shy on me now. You were an open book before, and I want to keep reading. Look at me. Thank you. Answer the question."

"Temptation is a beautiful thing."

"Tempting me will get you way more than you want."

She lay back on her elbows. "More than I want? I have been crushing on you for a long time. Shit. I have been daydreaming about you since I started at the station, boss man."

"Mr. boss man to you." She smiled. "You need to do that more often."

"Daydream about you?"

"No, smart ass, smile."

"I smile all the time."

"Yeah, but they're usually directed at someone else."

"No, you just aren't paying attention."

He pointed to the head of the bed. "Lie down before I change my mind and paddle that ass now."

She crawled to where he was directing her and flopped on to her back. "Stay with me?"

"I would like nothing more." By the time he shucked his jeans, lay in the bed and pulled the crumpled covers up from the foot of the bed, she was already snoring on her side, her ass pointing toward him. With an arm slung over her waist, he easily pulled her into him, her butt cradled in his groin. *Exactly where she belonged.*

A sudden, violent jerk ran through Gwen's body and forced Jensen from his sleep. If the movement had not woken him, the cry of pain that tore through the dark room would have. She was in pain, whether it was physical or emotional, he wasn't sure, but the glow from the street lamp outside her window left no doubt that her face was twisted and contorted with anguish.

"I'm sorry." The words were strangled; if he had not been paying such close attention to her, he may have missed them.

"Gwen, I'm here. You're safe. You're safe, bellissima." When she curled into him and rested her head on his shoulder, he let out a breath he had not been aware he was holding.

As he lay there, staring at the ceiling, questions ran through his mind. Was it just your run of the mill nightmare? Do they happen often? Was he making them worse?

With each question, he realized something. He needed to know more about this woman and he was excited to learn.

The alarm pulled him from his sleep. He reached to the nightstand and quickly silenced it. When the weight on his shoulder moved, he smiled and looked down at the wild mass of auburn curls sprayed across his grey shirt. He longed to feel it spread across his bare chest, to feel her breath warm his skin. He had every intention of waking her up; after all, she had her first spanking coming. But when he opened his eyes again, it was because her phone was blaring on the other side of the bed.

"Shit!" His arm was freed as she sat straight up in bed. "Shit." She grabbed her head and swayed a little bit, the hangover no doubt taking hold of her as a result of the sudden movement.

"Do you think your boss will let you call in hungover?"

She turned to him, managing to look as if she had forgotten he was there. "Umm, I don't know, will you?"

"Not a chance. Consider this your punishment for your excessive drinking."

"Going soft on me already?"

"No, I just decided that I would rather hold you this morning than spank you." He pulled her to him, taking her lips in a fierce kiss. When he pulled away, he rolled her slightly and landed a hard swat to her lace-covered ass. "Get in the shower, Gwen, before I start something we don't have the time to finish. I have to go home and get changed for work." He kissed her again. "I'll see you at the station." He smacked her ass again as he stood from the bed. He called her name as she rolled out of bed, his jeans half way up his thighs. "If you're late, I will drag your ass to the supply closet as soon as the morning meeting is over." As she ran to the bathroom, he chuckled, not sure if the threat was going to guarantee she was on time or late.

Chapter 6

"Have they gone through your laptop yet?"

Gwen looked up from her computer, a bit alarmed. "They're going to do that?"

"You connect to the station's network, don't you?"

"Yeah?"

"Then they are going to want to see it in order to rule out any outside devices."

Panic started to set in as her coworker walked away. This was her baby. She had never let anyone on to her computer, ever, and she didn't plan on starting any time soon. "Jensen!" She snagged his arm as he walked by. "They are going to go through my computer?"

The look on her face must have been more telling then she had intended. Instead of simply answering her question, he squatted in front of her, taking her hands in his. "They have to go through every computer that has connected to the network in the last six months, bellissima."

"But…" She swallowed hard. "This is.… I… my computer isn't clean. I mean, it's clean, but not *clean*."

The second the smirk spread across his face, she wanted to take the words back. "What sort of naughty thigs do you have on here? Anything I should know about?"

"No!"

"Your response was too quick for it to be the truth."

"Sir!" All conversation came to a halt as the alarm in the officer's voice registered throughout the room. "Sir, you need to see this!"

The other man had only gotten a few steps when the television clicked on and a grainy picture appeared. As the picture cleared, a silhouette of a man walked into the shot and took a seat on the previously unnoticed chair.

"How are you doing that?" Jensen asked as he looked between the television and the computer the officer sat in front of, both displaying the same thing.

"I'm not. I was tracking the user and I hit a worm, sir."

"A worm?"

Before it could be explained further, a computerized voice came through the speakers, "Detectives, it seems you were able to find the trail of bread crumbs I left for you." There wasn't a doubt in Gwen's mind that the man on the screen currently had a smug look on his darkened face. "Congratulations, you have made contact with 'the Hill City arsonist'." Every officer in the room jumped into action, some holding up phones and recording the video, others rushing to computers. "As I am sure the fine men of the Hill City Fire Department have already told you, they have nothing to do with the stalking of Sierra Boisy. Nor do I. However, the women of the department are the kings in *my* game and, as such, are to be protected at all costs. After all, if something happens to the kings, the game—our game—is over. I will not get into it any further than that, can't make your jobs too easy, now can I? But know this, gentlemen, protect those women. There is something much darker than me out there, and it is coming after them. Please heed my warnings, men. We can't leave the girls unprotected. I do not wish for this to get messy, and this mysterious, delinquent pawn is doing just that. The next play is yours. Check." With his final words, the screen went black.

A kiss was laid on the crown of her head as Jensen was summoned into his office and the whole room erupted in activity. This was the closest anyone had ever been to the arsonist, and no one was willing to let him get too far.

"Let's get out of this zoo before we are pulled in and never heard from again." Autumn grasped her hand, hauled her to her feet, dragging both her and Kennly down the hall.

"You mind telling me where we are going?"

"Narnia." She swung the door to the supply closet open and began pushing her way through the discarded items. "Leland decided that he was sick of me complaining about the scratchy couch back here, so he brought his from the basement. It's still a crap couch, but at least I can sit on it after." She paused and shot a quick look at Kennly. "At least I can sit on it."

"If you wanted the fact that you get your ass spanked on the regular, even at work, kept a secret, you shouldn't have shared so much with us at the bar last night."

Gwen paused at the line of bunker coats. "Are we doing the right thing?"

"What do you mean?" Autumn pushed the coats to the side and walked into the open space.

"I mean, there is an arsonist threatening us, our people, and the whole damn city and we are running away to, what, hide?"

"Who said anything about hiding?" Autumn flung herself down on the couch. "We're brainstorming."

Gwen sat on the other corner of the couch as Kennly pulled up a folding hair. "Nice. Maybe I will dig my other recliner out of storage."

"So there can be an audience to my demise? I don't think so."

"Something tells me you won't be the only one escorted to the supply closet in the future."

"Yeah?" All eyes landed on Gwen.

"Did you get down and dirty after our girls' night?" Kennly sat on the edge of her chair looking as if she was ready to take notes.

"Gossiping? What happened to the big brainstorm session you just justified our escape with?"

Both women shrugged. "We need to know all the dirty details first."

"Well, he drove me home and then held my hair while I prayed to the porcelain gods. I guess that counts as dirty details."

"You puked?"

"I think I got a little bit on him." Kennly threw her head back, a laugh escaping, as Autumn covered her face in an attempt to contain her snort. "It isn't funny. I had every intention of fucking him into a coma, but instead, I spent the night with my head in the toilet. Then he tucked me into bed like a perfect gentleman."

"That's it?"

"He cuddled me all night, but yeah, that was it."

"So, you guys aren't a thing?" questioned Autumn.

"No, we're most definitely a *thing*. There was never a question of that after our date, and if there was, the threat to my ass if I was late to work this morning cleared it all up."

"Ah, my little Gwenny is growing up."

Gwen tossed a discarded glove at Autumn's head. "Can we get back to the matter at hand, please? I know you have a plan in that head of yours, or we wouldn't be here."

"I do." She looked around the room like she expected someone to pop out as she started talking.

"Your boss is busy. You're safe for now."

"Until he finds out you intend to interfere in a police investigation." Gwen sat back on the couch and crossed her arms over her chest.

"Not interfering. Just helping."

Kennly grunted. "How, exactly, are we going to do that?"

"I have an old boyfriend. He's a fucking computer mastermind. He can literally do anything with the right equipment."

"Will he help us?"

Gwen watched as the woman next to her shrugged "I think so. He is always looking for a way to show off his talents."

"But? There has to be a but in there somewhere."

She took a deep breath before she continued. "He just got out of prison."

"What!" Gwen and Kennly both stared open mouthed at Autumn.

"It was only a year and not for anything bad. He was just caught hacking into a few databases he wasn't supposed to be in. Don't scuff at me, Gwendolyn. We can't just sit here and let this arsonist do God knows what until the nitwits the police have working for them decide to pull their heads out of their asses and admit that they are in way over their heads."

"She has a point."

"You're new, Kennly, so I will let you in on a well-known fact among the women in our group. You don't go along with Autumn's harebrained ideas unless you're willing to pay the price."

"But she has a good point. The guys out there are idiots. They had no idea that video was there. It was an accident they found it, and you know it."

"Or the arsonist decided he was sick of waiting and led them to it."

"Either way, we can't just sit here twiddling our thumbs. We have to do something."

"Yeah, tell the guys about this ex of yours and have them go through the right channels to get his help."

Autumn stood and started pacing the room. "The right channels will take too long. The longer this guy is out there, the braver he is going to get."

"And we know he isn't above killing anyone." Bile rose in the back of Gwen's throat as the sick feeling took over. Mentally shaking herself, she turned to the other women, her mind made up. "How do we do this?"

"Together," Kennly instantly responded. "We do this as one, or not at all."

"Are you kidding? One look at you, and he is going to run." At Kennly's questioning look, she continued. "You scream 'my dad's a cop.'."

"That's why we are doing it together. He knows you, so he won't freak. Gwen and I will be there to make sure you aren't in any danger. That's it."

"No. I have to do this on my own. He will trust me more than he ever will the two of you."

"You don't let us do this together, I will walk right out of this room and tell the men what we are plotting. Don't give me that look, Autumn. You know damn well I will do it."

"You do that, and the only option we will have left to us is to sit here and watch the cops flounder."

"If you have it your way, that is exactly what Gwen and I will be doing," Kennly pointed out.

"Sitting on the sidelines, going against everything Jensen and I have started, just to know you are safe is a risk I am willing to take if it means you aren't out there playing hero all by yourself. You can scowl at me all you want. It isn't going to change my mind. All of us, or none of us."

"Fine, but if the two of you mess this up, I'm doing it on my own."

"You can try, but I will run to Leland so fast it will make your head spin."

"I hate how stubborn you are." With a scowl, Autumn

flopped onto the couch, looking the part of a pouting child. "Now, all we have to do is find him."

"Give me his name. Don't worry, I won't go in by myself, but my dad's a cop, remember. I can get him to run the name and get his address."

"Colt Allander."

Chapter 7

The sound of the tone had Jensen groaning before he opened his eyes. "We have a report of a fire at 3425 Granger Avenue."

Jensen sat up and shoved his legs into his pants, pulling them up as he stood from the bed. He ran down the hall in his socks, the concrete floor cold against the soles of his feet. At his station issued SUV, he stepped into his bunker pants and boots in one smooth motion and watched the activity around him as he pulled them into place.

Men were coming from everywhere. The early risers were filing out of the kitchen, most with coffee in hand, men were descending the pole one after another, and a few stragglers were coming down the stairs, still buckling their belts.

Zander nudged Jensen as he ran past. "Only one good thing about this call."

"Right." No letter meant it wasn't the arsonist. Jensen shoved his arms into his coat, zipping it over his overalls. "A nice clean fire." Jensen climbed into his SUV, flipped a couple of switches to get the lights and sirens going, and was pulling out of the bay as he saw Gwen climb into the driver's seat of the ambulance.

When he finally pulled up to the building, the crowd had already started to gather. He jumped from his vehicle and headed over to an officer. "Abandoned?"

"Yeah. The registered owner lives in a different state. Neighbors haven't reported seeing any squatters, and we didn't see any evidence that suggested anything different. Snow was clean of footprints sans one set."

"And that one set?"

"Looked like someone tried to back track in their own steps, so we believe it to be empty."

Jensen nodded before turning his back to the officer and speaking into his mic as the trucks pulled up to the scene. "Looks like an abandoned building spitting out a bunch of smoke, so we are going to do a sweep. Ladder truck, get situated to enter from the top north corner, you're going to work your way down. Company One, you are going to enter from the front and work your way out and up. Company Two, open up some walls and get fans on this. I want to know where the smoke is coming from and then get it vented."

The activity around him would have looked a bit chaotic to anyone else, but to him, it was a well-planned and thought out process. They had trained countless times on this exact scenario. As he turned to the sound of a backup alarm, he watched as the girls situated the rig for a fast exit before they climbed out and readied their equipment for any possible patients.

He watched Zander help the other men with their tanks before he climbed onto the truck and started to position the ladder. As soon as it was in place, Leland and another man started climbing. That used to be him.

"You'll get used to it," Autumn said as she joined him. "I got used to seeing Lee disappear into the smoke, and you'll get used to seeing someone else do your old job."

"That obvious?"

"No, I just know how much you guys hate change, but Kevin

would not have picked you for captain if he hadn't thought you were going to be ready to fill his boots."

His radio crackled with, "We're entering the building, Chief."

"10-4, Boisy, keep your eyes open." He turned back to the medic at his side. "Thank you, Autumn. Now, get back to where you are supposed to be. You know you can't pass the line of trucks unless you have a full set of turnouts on."

Her bottom lip trembled slightly before she pressed them together in a thin line. "Yeah." As she blew out a shaky breath, she turned back to the rig. "We all know what happened last time."

He grabbed her arm and spun her back to face him. "Excuse me, medic?" When he was met with only silence, he continued. "I know your Dom would not be happy with that statement, Autumn."

"No, he wouldn't."

"Then why, sub?"

"It was out before I thought better of it, sir." He felt her cringe the slightest bit at the use of the formal title.

"As was that." He smiled at her before becoming serious again. "You either tell Leland about this, or I will. None of us want you to fall down that path again, and I have a feeling he knows how to keep that from happening."

Autumn groaned, her eyes dropping to his chest. "He does."

"I thought so." He released her and watched as she made her way back to the ambulance, where she was promptly bombarded with questions from Gwen.

Jensen turned back to the building in front of him. Autumn was right. He missed his old job. He missed going into smoke filled buildings to discover the unknown, but he also respected the new ranking his old friend had honored him with.

In Hill City, the ranking of captain was a position no one knew they had until it was needed. Each chief gave it to a lieutenant they believed would be able to fill their shoes in the event of a sudden crippling illness or death. It is then up to the lieutenant whether they accept the position or not. It was a probationary position for six months, and then the board decided if they stayed in place or hired another man for the job.

When Jensen found out he had been honored with the ranking, it was bittersweet, but he had accepted the new rank in an instant. He was going to do everything he could to prove Kevin had made the right choice.

"Chief, we found the source of the smoke. Small fire on the second floor. We were able to dowse it and will be continuing our search for occupants."

"10-4. Company Two, did you copy? I want those fans going and the smoke cleared out!"

"Chief?" A feminine voice came over the radio.

"Go ahead, Gwen."

"We need you at the ambulance."

That statement was all it took to get his hunches up. He moved swiftly through the crowd of people and scattered equipment to the rig. "What's wrong."

The girls turned to him, Gwen handing him a pair of gloves. "When we went to start the paperwork, this was taped to the computer. It's addressed to you, and it hasn't been there long."

Jensen donned the gloves and took the paper from Gwen before digging his phone out of his pocket and making a quick call. Once his phone was safely back where it belonged, he spoke into the mic secured to his shoulder, "Fire Chief Keetes to dispatch."

"This is dispatch; go ahead, Chief."

"Can you send a couple more officers to my location, please, and the detectives handling the arsonist case if possible. I'll be talking with the medics when they get here."

"10-4."

He had to resist the urge to crumple the paper into a small ball as he read it.

. . .

Chief Keetes,

It seems to me that we have had what I would call a breakdown in communication. You see, this is my *fire, but no one bothered to tell you, did they?*

How are you to properly protect the queens if you are not kept in the loop? Better yet, how is my story *meant to be told if the higher ups are not following the rules?*

You should have been told the second the fire marshal got my letter. However, PD was too busy playing with your computers to bring you into the fold.

If they don't follow the rules, I am going to have to get creative on how I punish these transgressions. Unfortunately, it will be the girls who pay the price.

Now, Chief Keetes, I suggest you get your ducks in a row.

Don't worry, I will keep in touch.

"What seems to be the problem, Chief?"

It took every ounce of self-control Jensen had not to punch the pompous, overweight detective in the throat. "Got here pretty quickly for this being a run of the mill fire, didn't you, Starling?"

"You called us over here, Chief. I am guessing, by now, you have figured out that this is the work of the arsonist."

"Damn right, I have! Do you know how much danger you have put everyone here in?"

"I don't, because no one was in any danger. We had at least ten undercover cops in that crowd." Starling gestured to the growing number of people on the other side of the police tape.

"Then why the hell aren't they doing their jobs? My medics found this on their laptop." When the detective tried to grab the paper from Jensen, he pulled away. "No, I don't trust you or your minions with this."

Venom dripped from every word he spewed, "If you don't give me the evidence, I will have you charged with obstruction of justice so fast your head will spin!"

"Try it, Starling. You see, I called a friend of mine. You may know him, actually, Atticus Pardoe." Jensen smiled when he saw said man approaching out of the corner of his eye.

"You called my supervisor? What gives you the fucking right to go over my head?"

"I suggest you stop talking, Starling.

"You have got to be fucking kidding!"

"Far from it. I have a stack of complaints sitting on my desk right now, so do yourself a favor and just walk away. I will handle this one," Atticus growled.

Starling glared at Jensen but did as he was told. "He is right, you know. Going over his head could have been bad for you. You're lucky I have a mutual dislike for him. I don't care how it could have gone for me." Jensen looked to the medics. "My only concern is that my people are safe while they do their jobs. Detective Starling is keeping me from being able to do that."

"It wasn't his call."

"Ultimately, I'm sure it wasn't, but I have no doubt he put the bug in their ear. Your poker face needs work."

Atticus sighed in defeat. "Okay, you have proven to everyone watching that you have the balls for your new ranking, so tell me, why I am here, rather than hitting the snooze button on my alarm clock a few more times?" Jensen handed Atticus the letter and watched the emotions as they ran across his face. Shock, distain, anger. "Looks like this guy wants to show everyone how big his balls are, too."

"What do you mean, this isn't from the arsonist?" Jensen stood from his chair, the force of his movement bouncing it off the wall behind him.

"The techs and I have been all over this letter and compared it to everything we have from the arsonist. This isn't his."

"How do you know?"

"The wording is wrong." Atticus held up the sealed plastic bag containing the letter. "We have every reason to believe the video from this morning was authentic, and while the person who wrote this got some of the references correct, others were obviously wrong."

"He called the girls queens." Jensen rubbed his temples as the reality of the situation set in.

"Exactly. The man in the video said they were the kings in his game and, as such, they needed to be protected. Here," he passed the letter to Jensen, pointing at the mistake, "he refers to them as queens. In the game of chess, queens are not protected."

"They are feared."

"Feared?" Leland questioned as he paced the room, his hair disheveled from running his fingers through it.

"In chess, the queen can move in any direction at any time. If used correctly, they can clear the board of all the other pieces."

"The fire bug messed up his references in his haste to write it, so what?"

"It's more than that. In the video, he said we needed to protect the women. Why would he say that and then turn around, not even twelve hours later, and threaten them?"

"He has never threatened them before?" Jensen watched as the emotions moved across the other man's face.

"Never."

"Finally, our arsonist is past the small barrel fire that produces lots of smoke stage. He has worked his way up to full-blown, life-threatening fires, and he isn't going back. He can't. They won't satisfy his need any longer."

"What are you saying?" The question didn't need to be asked.

Everyone in the room knew, but the need to hear the words was great.

"We have a copycat." The room erupted in curses. Jensen's fists bounced off the massive desk. Leland collapsed into a chair, his elbows on his knees and his hands steepled between his legs. Atticus wasn't done. ""Other than the people who were in the room when the clip played, only three other people saw the video. Those three were all accounted for and miles away when the letter was put in the rig."

A harsh laugh huffed from Jensen's chest. "That means it's an inside job."

"This information does not get shared with anyone. We cannot risk this getting back to him. It would be catastrophic."

Chapter 8

"I don't think I have ever needed coffee this badly in my life." The hot mug warmed Gwen's cold fingers as she brought it to her lips. She was still chilled from spending all morning in the cold March weather.

As she relaxed into her seat, she watched Autumn take a seat across from her. "I can already taste the bacon."

"I have to use the john. I'll be right back."

Autumn turned to Gwen as soon as the man was out of sight. "Leland is trying to decide if we should cancel tonight."

"Cancel what?"

A wicked smile spread across the other woman's face. "We are hosting a get together at our house tonight. You should come."

She eyed the woman across from her suspiciously. "What are you up to?"

Before Gwen could get more information out of her, Jensen walked up to the table. "Where's Boisy?"

"Bathroom," they both responded at the same time.

"Stay here," he commanded as he, too, walked away.

"Are they going to be this bossy all the time?"

"That depends."

"On what?"

"Two things, really. How freaked out they are over the arsonist's announcement, and whether or not this is what you want."

"This is absolutely what I want." It was Gwen's turn to smile. "I haven't gotten a chance to explore with him yet, but I have a feeling that is going to change. If I have my way, it will be sooner, rather than later."

"I could help with that. Come to the house tonight. We're going to play cards, and there's always room for more." At her questioning look, Autumn continued. "Everyone who is going to be there are people who practice the same lifestyle we do. Not anything intentionally kinky, but it never stays vanilla for long."

"I'll ask Jensen about it. God knows I'm dying to see his secrets."

"Me, too!" She sipped her coffee with a faraway look in her eyes. "Now, you *have* to come."

The men stepped up to the table before she could respond. "It isn't up to you, princess. That is up to her and her Dom."

"Scoot in, bellissima."

"Please goes a long way there, boss man."

"Yet you started sliding over without thought." He smiled at her once more before turning to the other couple and allowing his expression to become serious.

"Can we order breakfast before everyone goes somber?" Autumn asked as she rubbed her belly. "Standing around, watching you guys fight a fire takes a lot out of a woman."

"We already ordered." With a deep breath, he jumped right in. "We're worried. The arsonist confirmed yesterday morning that he has special interest in the two of you, and we don't want to take any chances."

"You mean, last night?"

The men shared a look. "Exactly."

"We need to know the two of you are safe."

"While a leave of absence would—"

"No!" both women interrupted at the same time.

"Princess, listen."

"Don't 'princess' her. You knew we would never agree to give up our jobs, even temporarily."

"Gwen, that—"

"How dare you guys even suggest this? If it were you two being targeted, this wouldn't even be a suggestion."

"Gwendolyn."

The growled warning made her pause for a second before she added, "No. You don't get to use my full name and think I am just going to quietly do as I'm told. Fuck that."

Before she knew what was happening, she was hauled across the booth seat, pulled to her feet and guided to the back of the restaurant.

Once in the privacy of the back-hall, Jensen spun her around to face him before pinning her to the wall with a hand planted on either upper arm. Stuck. "You never being in a relationship like this before is the only reason I am not taking you back to my house to roast your ass right now." He placed his pointer finger over her mouth. "Not a word, Gwendolyn. We will talk about this later, but for right now, we will go back out there and finish the conversation we were having, and you will listen to what we have to say before you start popping off at the mouth and assuming you know what we are talking about. And when you do speak, you will do so respectfully."

"Yes, Sir," tumbled from her mouth as a feeling of belonging fell over her and she relaxed into his hold.

"Let's go eat breakfast." He planted a kiss to the top of her head before landing a swat to her ass and leading her back to the table.

"Well, she didn't flinch when she sat down, so that's a good sign," Autumn stage whispered as Gwen slid into the booth and picked up her fork, eyeing the fresh stack of pancakes.

Leland chucked. "Mind your own business. If they wanted you to know what happened, they would tell you, snoopy sub."

Jensen placed his hand on Gwen's thigh and gave it a tender squeeze as he poured syrup over his own stack. "Go on, Boisy, she may actually let you finish a sentence this time."

"I'm not going to lie. I would love for both of you to be as far away from this as possible, but I know that is not a rational decision and definitely not one Jensen and I can make for you." He smiled at the woman next to him. "Even if it would put our minds at ease, we know that's not what you would want."

"Oh." Gwen looked down at her plate, pancakes still untouched.

"We have a few ideas on how to keep you guys better protected, and one of them will be put into effect as soon as we can set it up."

"Will we be kept in the loop about what this plan is when it comes time to implement it?"

"Yes," both men stated at the same time. The lack of hesitation had Gwen relaxing into her seat.

"Okay," Gwen started as she shoved a piece of bacon in her mouth.

"Now, on to more important things." Autumn paused dramatically. "What time are you guys going to be at the house tonight?"

"I thought Leland's house was in the country?" Gwen questioned as they pulled into the driveway of a small cottage only a few blocks from the station.

"This is my place. We'll go to Boisy's later. Right now, we're going to deal with what went down at the diner. For that, we need privacy. There is no reason for prying eyes to see me take my displeasure out on your ass. For this first time, anyway."

Before Gwen could protest, Jensen was out of his truck and rounding the hood.

"You could have at least given me the chance to argue with you," Gwen mumbled as he helped her from the truck. "And what do you mean by 'first time'?"

He slapped her ass. "I figured I could save us both the trouble, but if you really want to argue, we can." He led her through the garage and to a side door of the house, swinging it open and allowing her to go first. "Why do you sound too excited about the prospect of someone seeing me correct you, bellissima."

She quickly looked around the small, inviting kitchen before turning back to Jensen, her bravado gone. "I don't want to argue, but we do need to talk."

"The words every man dreads to hear."

"It isn't anything bad. I just, I think my innocent act these last couple of years has led you to believe that I am more naive that I truly am."

"Gwen." He grabbed her hand and led her to a dining room, pushing her into a chair. He crouched before her. The concern etched in his face had Gwen wishing she could take back her words. "So, your inexperienced and new to this type of relationship. It's not—"

"But I'm not."

"Not?"

"I'm not inexperienced or new to this type of relationship, Jensen. I grew up with this type of relationship. While my parents tried to keep it discreet, I knew." She watched his face closely as she spoke her next words. "I have also had a couple of relationships like this. Not successful ones, obviously, but I was the sub to their Dom, and I loved every minute of it."

"Then why act like all things lifestyle were foreign concepts to you for so long?"

"To make myself believe I didn't need it."

"One of them hurt you?"

She picked at her nails.

"What happened?"

"He started topping another woman. By the time he told me about her, he was in love, and I was devastated." She swallowed hard and forced herself to continue. "We were in deep. Damn near Master/slave and then it was just over. Looking back, she fit into his kinks far better than I did, but by the time I realized that, the damage was done. I started having nightmares, and I decided that playing the vanilla was better than going through that heartbreak again."

"The nightmare last night?"

"Yeah, but for the first time ever, it had a different, better ending. It had closure."

He squeezed her hand reassuringly. "So, when I said that I wasn't going to blister your ass right then because you were new to the lifestyle?"

"I tried to tell you."

"And I wouldn't let you." He stood and pulled her into his arms. "I'm sorry. I will be better about letting you tell me stuff in the future. I promise."

"That is all I can ask for. Thank you."

"You know what this means though, right?"

"You're going to let me off the hook?"

Jensen laughed as he took her place in the chair. "Nice try, bellissima. I did that yesterday morning and look at where we are now. Pants down."

"Why do you keep calling me that?"

He watched her face as she undid her jeans. "It suits you."

"It's more than that, isn't it?" She wiggled her jeans down her hips, allowing them to pool at her feet before she kicked them away.

He smiled. "It's what my dad has always called my mom."

"So, you just stole your dad's pick-up line?" Her hand landed on her hips as a smirk split her face.

"You're standing in front of me in only your underwear; it really takes all the power out of your stance, you know."

She let her hands drop. "I'm a little rusty in my submission."

"Let's see if we can remedy that." He leaned back in the chair, giving her the room necessary to lay herself across his lap. "Panties down first."

Unceremoniously, she shoved her underwear down and moved to his right side. She didn't hesitate in laying herself across his lap; there was no point. She wanted to submit.

His ran his hands over her nates, admiring the goose bumps that formed. "I believe you should start as you intend to finish."

She looked at him through her stray curls. "What does that mean?"

"It means I don't believe in warm ups."

"Ever?"

"Unless I am using an implement. In that case, I will use my hand first."

"Is this one of those times?"

"No, bellissima. I will only be using my hand for this one. Are you ready?"

She looked at the floor before she spoke again. "Are there any rules during punishment that I should know about?"

"Never reach back. You can swear and be as loud you want, but there is to be no name-calling and no swearing at me. Do you know the difference between swearing and swearing *at* me?" When she nodded her head, he continued. "Explain, please."

"I cannot use any swear words when answering your questions or addressing you."

"Good girl. Any more questions before I start?" When there was no response, he laid down a hard spank. "You said yourself that you are not new to the scene, so I assume you know how to answer me when I ask you a question, especially while you're in this position."

"No, Sir, I don't have any questions." He wasted no more time, landing swat after swat on her tender flesh.

"Holy shit!" His previous statement rang true as his hand bounced off her nates, the spanks hard and fast right from the start. Numerous swats landed in one spot before he deemed it fit to move on to a new location. She was just starting to wiggle when the lecture started.

"Why are you here, bellissima?"

"I jumped to conclusions and interrupted you and Leland."

After a second, he moved his hands to the tops of her thighs. "You forgot one."

She scrambled to come up with what he wanted. "I can't think when you spank there, Sir."

"Maybe you can think better when I turn my attention elsewhere then." The assault on her thighs stopped, but she knew her reprieve would be short lived. "Spread your legs." She did as she was told and the slap to her inner thighs was a shock. "Not where you thought my hand was going, huh? I will keep at this tender skin until I get what I want."

"Please, Sir, it hurts. I can't think."

"I had you explain the rule to me before your spanking started. There it is; she remembers now."

"I swore at you. I'm sorry, Sir."

"It was very *rude,* wasn't it?"

"Shit! Yes, Sir! I was rude. I'm sorry."

"Which one of the D's does it break?"

"Disrespect, Sir. I broke the rule about respecting you. I'm sorry!"

"Now, sub, I know you know that that little apology isn't going to cut it, don't you?"

She wiggled as his hand rubbed and soothed the warm flesh he had just painted red with his attention. His fingers grazed her labia right before he pulled his hand away and he started pelting her sit spots. "No. I mean, I know, Sir, but my butt is not the leather ass it once was."

He chuckled as he moved up to her ass once more before starting the trip down to her thighs and back up. "Then I suggest you behave until we get your ass up to par."

He didn't talk any more as he focused on her full, rounded bottom. While it did not hurt as much as the previous bout, the buildup had done its job and she could do nothing to stop the tears from gathering. She didn't want to cry. Hell, she had taken more than this and not shed a tear, but, somehow, this was different.

"Let go, bellissima."

"I can't." Her voice broke.

"You need this. Trust me, I promise to catch you."

The tender truth in his words was her undoing. The tears ran down her face, dripping off the end of her nose in fast succession. Ten more strikes of his hand landed before she went limp over his lap and his tempo slowed. "I'm sorry, Sir." She hiccupped a bit as he flipped her over and carried her in his arms to the sofa. "I don't remember a hand hurting so much before."

"Leather butt only lasts if you use it." He situated her on the couch next to him with her head in his lap before he tossed a blanket over her lower half. "Wasted too much time pretending to be what you're not. All your resilience is long gone, bellissima."

She huffed a laugh. "Trust me, I know, but it is worth it when this is the result. This is my favorite part."

"You mean when I don't try to pull your hair out?"

She laughed while he untangled his fingers from her locks and started rubbing her back. With every pass he made up her back, the weight of her guilt ebbed, and the weight of her eyelids grew. Soon, she was drifting somewhere between sleep and wakefulness.

There were ten minutes of silence, neither willing to break the spell that the aftercare had on them before his phone rang.

When he didn't make a move to answer it, her heart swelled. Without opening her eyes, she asked, "Aren't you going to get that?"

"No, I have an answering machine. Besides, this is my favorite part, too."

"Me, nearly comatose on your lap?"

"No, you all compliant and purring. You, still being naked under that blanket isn't all that bad, either."

She sat up so she could see the smug look on his face. "Compliant? Are you saying that I am too much for you?"

"Never, I am just learning that you are not as docile as you liked to make everyone believe." He scooped her into his arms again as he slid down the sofa and stretched out on his back. When they were finally settled, she was wedged between his side and the back of the couch, safe, warm, and content. With her head on his chest, she fell asleep to the steady beat of his heart under her ear.

Chapter 9

A content mewl rumbled from Gwen's chest when his hand roamed over her hip and across her ass before fingers softly glided up the crease of her butt and down again, only to repeat the pattern. She was fully on top of him, having moved in her sleep, her chest pressed against his, his hard cock pressing into her belly.

He grabbed her ass, forcing a moan from her lips. As he released her tender flesh, he started the trek over her ass again, but this time when he moved down the seam in her ass, she slightly spread her legs in a silent invitation.

"Say it," he commanded, pausing in his ministrations. "I won't give it to you unless you ask."

"Please touch me." He didn't hesitate. As soon as the words were out, he pushed his fingers lower, caressing the warm lips of her pussy. She opened her legs wider and attempted to push back on his fingers.

The phone ringing startled her awake, chasing away the perfect dream. "Sorry, bellissima." Jensen reached for the phone. "Hey, Mom."

She lifted her head from his chest, wiped at her mouth with

the back of her hand and stood from the couch, her bladder demanding attention. When she returned, Jensen was just ending the call. "How long did we sleep?"

"About three and a half hours. How's your butt?"

"It isn't sore any longer." He pulled her toward him before he fisted the flesh of her right ass cheek, causing her to squirm and moan. "Well, when you do that."

While he groaned in return, he released her cheek. "As much as I would love for you to stay in your half-dressed state, you need to get the rest of your clothes on. I forgot about my promise to go see my parents. I'll take you home on the way. What's wrong?"

As she tried to school her features, she shrugged. "Nothing."

"Oh, no." She didn't even get one step toward her discarded clothing before she was pulled into his lap. "You're very close to breaking one of our rules."

"But."

"We both know it's not nothing. Be honest and tell me what had you looking so disappointed."

"I was looking forward to spending time with you."

"With just me?"

"No. I suppose I can share you." She laughed at his affronted look. "I just wanted to spend some more time with you away from the station and not hindered by alcohol. You know, as just Gwen and Jensen. Some place where I don't have to keep people alive and you aren't the boss of everyone."

"Where I am just the boss of you?"

"No. Yes." She rolled her eyes. "I don't know. I was just looking forward to a night of us and whatever we decided to do."

"Okay. Get dressed. We're going to my parents' house."

"Maybe this wasn't such a good idea," Gwen mumbled as they turned on the gravel road that led to his parents' place. "We've only gone on one date, hardly serious enough to meet the parents."

When he pulled the truck to the side of the road, Jensen put it into park. Not taking his eyes off the steering wheel, he spoke. "You're right. I would never introduce a girl to my parents this soon in a normal relationship. Hell, I've *never* introduced a girl to my parents." He turned to her. "But I have also never had a snowball fight on a first date. Or needed to protect another woman as fiercely as I do you. This isn't a normal relationship. You're different, we are different, and neither one of us is taking this lightly. This isn't some carefree fling. There's a lot at stake here. I'm your boss, and you're one of the best medics in Hill City. I put a lot of thought into how this would work before I ever started entertaining the idea of us as a couple."

He grasped her chin, forcing her to look at him. "I'm not telling you this to make you cry." He wiped the single tear from her face. "I am telling you this because you need to know that you are not just another notch on my bedpost. If I didn't intend for this to work and to fight like hell to make it permanent, I would never have started pursuing you all those months ago. And I guess if that scares you off then, at least, I can look back and say I tried."

She didn't have words, so she did the next best thing. She wrapped her arms around his neck and pulled him in for a hard, passionate kiss, which they were still enjoying five minutes later when there was a knock on the window.

"You know, I really thought the last time I would catch you necking a girl in your pick-up at the end of the drive, would have been years ago, but here we are, reliving old times."

Tearing her lips away, Gwen buried her face in her hands. "Oh my God! Please kill me now."

Jensen chuckled as he rolled down his window. "Dad."

"Jensen, and you must be Gwen." Gwen had no choice but to shake his outstretched hand. "Greg Keetes. Now, the two of you get to the house before your mother paces a hole in the front rug, will you? I'm right behind you." He took a step back from the truck.

As soon as the truck was rolling, and the window was up, Gwen slugged Jensen in the arm. "Your dad just caught us making out in your truck like a couple of teenagers."

"I know, babe, I was there, but if you hit me again, he will see me painting your ass a beautiful shade of red. Maybe I could get it about the same color as your face right now."

The truck wasn't even in park before the front door swung open and a petite woman stepped out. "Shit, do you think she saw us, too?"

He turned to her. "Gwen, I am thirty-five-years-old. If I want to kiss my girl in my truck until her toes curl, then I am damn well going to do just that."

Chapter 10

He was so proud of her. The blush hadn't completely dissipated yet, but Gwen strolled confidently up to his mom and introduced herself. When the shock of her only son bringing a woman home finally wore off, he watched as his mom wrapped his girl in her arms.

"Daniella, if you don't let that girl go, we are never going to get her to come back."

"You don't have to worry about that; I would always come back to see George."

"You've met George?"

Jensen huffed a laugh. "Met? She tried to turn your dog against me."

Gwen whirled on him, hands propped on her hips, sass dripping from every word. "I did no such thing! I simply used him to distract you, so I could build up a suitable amount of ammunition to pelt you in the head with."

When he snagged her by the elbow to pull her out of his mother's arms and into his chest, he said, "I think you just told my parents of your plot to kill me."

Horror crossed her face as she realized how her words must

have sounded to them. Laughter rumbled through him as her head fell to his chest, but it was only there for a second before she straightened her spine and turned to his parents once more. "We had a snowball fight in the middle of the night, in your back yard. It was our first date."

His mother laughed as she looped her arm through Gwen's and led her into the house. "Come on; I have to get to know the woman who has my son tied in knots."

"I'm not so sure about that, Mrs. Keetes."

"Call me Daniella, and trust me, Jensen is smitten."

While he stood in the cold on his parents' front porch, he looked to his laughing dad. "I'm not sure what just happened."

"Your mom just claimed that girl as her own. If you don't marry her, she's going to adopt her."

"I could not imagine doing what you do. All the blood and gore."

Jensen chuckled at his mom's shiver.

"It isn't that bad, and the adrenaline makes it easier."

"A bit of an adrenaline junky?"

"I am, Mr. Keetes."

"Greg."

"Sorry, Greg."

"Your blush is showing again, bellissima." The sharp intake of breath from across the table caught Jensen's attention. "Ma, it isn't that big of a deal."

She waved him off before turning to Gwen. "Did you know that bellissima is what his father calls me?"

"I did."

"Do you know why he calls me that?"

"Because you're beautiful?"

"Yes," both Jensen and his father proclaimed at the same time, daring the older woman to disagree.

Jensen watched his mom roll her eyes. "He also calls me that because I'm Italian. My parents moved here shortly before I was born. The little bit of English they could speak was very broken and hard to understand, even after years of my siblings and me trying to teach them. The first time Greg met them, my father had practiced what he was going to say for hours. He was determined to be able to carry on a conversation with him. He wanted to get to know the man." She turned and smiled at her husband. "What my father and I didn't know, at the time, was that Greg had been practicing as well. Unfortunately for him, he had been doing so with his cousin. Long story short, he ended up slaughtering whatever it was that he was trying to say."

"I wanted to tell him that I loved his beautiful daughter with all my heart and to ask him for her hand in marriage."

"The only word he got correct was bellissima. For the rest of the night, both he and my father called me that. It was a real boost to a girl's ego."

"And it stuck. I have been calling her that ever since." He chuckled. "The only time I call her Daniella is when she's in trouble."

Gwen laughed at what Jensen knew was his pained expression before she smiled evilly at him. "Sounds like father, like son."

With a growl, he playfully pinched her thigh. "Except I know more than one word of Italian." His next words were for her ears only. "Like sculacciata." He nipped her lobe before he looked to his mother.

"You should; I drilled it into all of you kids when you were younger. I wanted you to know some of your past."

"Not to mention, every time they got under her skin, her words became a jumble of English and Italian. I don't know how many times I heard her threaten to give them a sculacciata with her spoon for their cattivo behavior."

Gwen turned her big eyes on him. She had filled in the blanks and had figured out exactly what sculacciata was. When she turned back to their hosts, she spoke to his mother. "When he told me it was his father's pet name for you, I knew it had more meaning than he was letting on. I love when he calls me bellissima. It makes my heart light."

"It was a part of his childhood that he wishes to carry into his future, and he chose you to do that with." Daniella smiled at the two of them.

Deciding to turn the topic of conversation, Greg asked. "So, you are on the same shift as Jensen?"

"Yep. Have been, for about four years now."

"So you knew the previous chief as well?"

"Yeah, he hired me." Gwen looked to the floor. "I had nine job interviews all over the state and I was ready to give up. At my tenth interview, what I had decided would be my last, he took a chance on the female medic; I owe him so much." Jensen took stock of the woman at his side. Sadness shone in her eyes, but so did her unwavering determination. "I will do everything in my power to help catch the fucking bastard who killed him." Her eyes widened slightly. "Sorry, I just…I should have chosen to word that differently."

"I agree wholeheartedly." His mother held up her hand, keeping Jensen from speaking. "Not that you should have watched your mouth. Fucking bastard were the exact words you needed to use. Oh, Greg, don't look at me like that. What else am I to call the person deliberately putting the life of my son in danger. His job is dangerous enough, now some 'fucking bustard' is targeting them."

A snort of laughter erupted from Gwen, forcing Jensen's brow to quirk. "I'm sorry. I tried to stop it, but swear words coming from your sweet, innocent mom is hilarious." As he squeezed her knee gently, he turned to his dad.

"Daniella, it has warmed up a bit, and I think that dog of yours wants out."

"That is code for 'go do something productive before I decide to get bossy.'." Want to walk with me to the mail box?"

"Yeah, probably in my best interests, too."

As soon as the women shut the door behind them, his dad said, "And that is how she is going to get all the dirty details out of your girl."

Jensen shrugged. "She may just get more information than she bargained for."

"Think she already has a plan in place to 'help' catch this arsonist of yours?"

"Without a doubt." When his father raised his brow, he shrugged. "I have to trust that if she needs me, she will come to me."

"And if she doesn't?"

"She has been on her own for a long time, dad. It's a new relationship. Hell, we have only been on one date, but I trust her. If she gets overwhelmed, she will come to me." He ran his hand over his bald head. "And if she puts herself in danger, she and I will address it."

"Get her to talk to you, son. I would put money on that woman already having a plan in motion."

The conversation had taken a turn to easier topics when his mom came into the house alone. "Where's Gwen?"

As sheepishly as he had ever seen her, his mother looked between the two of them before his dad spoke. "Just tell me that whatever it is doesn't require a trip to the hospital."

With a huff and a roll of her eyes, she finally looked at Jensen. "Don't listen to your father; it's not that bad."

Jensen was out of his chair and at the door to the garage in a heartbeat. "Gwendolyn."

He heard her laugh before she stepped from around the truck, the fabric of her shirt dangling uselessly in front of her, exposing the left side of her chest. "I need your shirt."

"What happened?" He fingered the flap of material before he

ran his finger over her exposed flesh, her belly contracting under his hand.

"George took off running."

He huffed a laugh. "That's why mom looked like a child caught with her hand in the cookie jar."

When he didn't elaborate, she continued. "He went into the thick of trees behind the house. We went after him, of course, but I was lucky enough to get my shirt caught on one of the left-over nails from, what your mom says, used to be a tree house. Now, give me your shirt." All it took was an arch of his brow to remind her who she was talking to, and her eyes instantly dropped to her toes. "Please, Sir?"

He pulled his shirt over his head before popping her on the ass. "Manners go a long way." After he dropped the shirt into place, he turned to the door, sticking his head inside. "We're going to head out."

His dad just laughed as he waved them off. He took Gwen's hand in his as he led her to his truck. "Shit, it's cold. Maybe I should have brought a coat after all."

"I can give you back your shirt."

"Take that shirt off, and we are going to be doing much more than kissing in this driveway. It won't just be my chest that's cold, either."

The feel of her finger tracing the thick, black line of the tattoo circling his arm had his dick twitching behind his zipper. "I'll make you a deal. I'll let you take full inventory of my chest—"

"And all your tattoos."

"And all my tattoos, *if* you wear my shirt to for the rest of the day."

"Deal! Wait, are we going anywhere special?"

"Just to Boisy's house."

"Deal!" With a satisfied expression, she managed to finagle her own shirt out from under his before tossing the torn garment into the back seat. "I had every intention of making you freeze anyway."

"Just so you could look at my tattoos?"

"Among other things. How long have you had them?"

He smiled, knowing exactly what she was talking about. "About five years now." As soon as the words were out of his mouth, he felt the slight tug on his nipple as her fingers wrapped around the silver hoop, admiring his piercing.

"Thank God. I wasn't sure if I could have left them alone long enough to heal if you had told me they were new."

At a stop sign, he turned and clasped her chin in his hand. "Maybe you should get yours done so we can match, then I'll have something to play with."

"Maybe we already match."

Chapter 11

"I'm not complaining about the view or anything, but did I give the impression that this was a clothing optional get together?" Autumn questioned from across the table, a smirk playing on her lips.

"Keep admiring a man that isn't me, princess, and you may be the next one without clothes."

Gwen eyed the others over her cards. "I tore my shirt before we came over, and he was nice enough to give me his."

"Last shirt you had, huh?" Liv laughed at her own joke. "Now you guys can stop pestering me about his tattoos. Did they hurt?"

"The tattoos or the piercings?"

"The nipples."

"Just the clamps," Gwen answered at the same time Jensen did. All the eyes in the room swung to her. "Gin!" she called as she laid her cards down on the table and started to rise from her seat. A hand clamped on her leg, stopping her escape, but it was everyone staring at her that had her dropping her eyes and smiling to herself.

"We aren't even playing Gin."

Sierra's confusion had Gwen snorting a laugh. "I know."

"Can I see?"

"Liv, you've seen pierced nipples before." She pointedly looked at the man next to her.

"So."

With a smile, Gwen whispered in Jensen's ear, enjoying his need to crudely adjust himself under the table far too much. "You're not going to get any complaints out of me."

"I didn't think I would." She addressed the table, "New game! If you guys can beat me at poker, I will show you my piercings."

"Strip poker?" Sierra stood from the table. "I'm out. Bye guys."

She eyed the others. "Last chance to back out if you're not up for the challenge."

"I'm in," Liv announced as she tossed her cards onto the table, forgetting the game they were previously playing.

"Lee?"

He smiled at his girlfriend. "Oh, we are definitely in."

Autumn's happy dance was interrupted by a deep voice from the hall. "Sorry I'm late. People do stupid shit at the worst times."

"Atticus. I was beginning to wonder if you were going to make it." Leland stood and greeted the officer. "You're just in time."

He took the only open seat and nudged Liv with his elbow. "What are we playing, lovie?"

"Strip poker."

"Jensen losing?"

"No, he showed up that way. Something about running out of shirts. I don't know, I was too distracted to listen." Autumn laughed at her joke until Leland nipped her ear teasingly.

"You really know how to make a man self-conscious."

"Rules. The player who didn't fold, with the worst hand of the round loses an article of clothing. If you run out of clothing to discard, you are not allowed to quit the game. Instead, your

Dom or sub or other unattached player…" She looked to Liv for approval of this statement. At her eager nod, she finished, "… gets to draw a punishment." She snagged a pad of paper from the counter. "Each of us gets to write three. Ladies, we write punishments for the men. Men, you write them for the girls. Be nice, guys."

"I don't see this going too well for us," Liv mumbled as she scribbled on her paper.

"Come on, how bad can it be? Besides, most of us have seen the others in action before. I can't count how many times I have seen your ass." Liv wagged her tongue at the other woman. "I've seen that with a clothespin on it, too."

When the laughter died, Gwen said, "You can take off your clothing in any order you want. Jensen gets one free pass because I stole his shirt. And lastly, socks as a pair are one article."

Jensen simply smiled at her as he dealt the cards. "Let's see if we can get some clothes off my girl, shall we?"

"I've taken some off."

"Your socks hardly count."

"She took off her bra, too, remember?" Liv smiled at the man innocently.

The groan that vibrated from Jensen's chest had a smirk playing on Gwen's lips. "How could I forget? She pulled it out from under her shirt without even a glimpse of the beautiful skin beneath." He shook his head disapprovingly.

"Not to mention the pebbled nipples trying their best to force their way through her shirt for the last fifteen minutes." Leland dodged the ice cube as it soared past his head.

"Not helping." At Jensen's complaint, Gwen smiled innocently. "Don't give me that look, or I will pull you over my lap for more swats. No pouting, bellissima."

"But I'm winning. How come I keep getting spanked?"

"Because you're winning," the guys proclaimed as one.

"It's totally killing her not to roll her eyes right now." The ice cube Gwen threw hit its mark and rested nicely on the front clasp of Autumn's exposed bra, the only article of clothing she had left. Smiling, she popped the cube into her mouth and spoke around it. "Nice shot."

Gwen gave her cards a quick glance and laid them down as she looked around the table. "I'll take three." After looking at the new cards, she shrugged. "I'll stay."

"There's that naughty smirk of yours."

"What smirk?"

"The smirk that never bodes well for your ass. " After taking his own cards, Jensen said, "Show us what you got."

Gwen flipped her cards, revealing her hand. "Three of a kind. King high."

"You've got the low hand; strip."

"How do you—" She didn't need to finish her statement as the rest of the players laid down their hands. "Cheaters!"

"Prove it."

"You all have straights, what other evidence do I need?" Her mouth fell open as realization dawned. "You guys let them cheat? What happened to subbies sticking together?"

"Let them?" Liv didn't get any further before Atticus reached over and pinched her thigh. An obvious order to keep quiet. "Coincidence."

"Coincidence, my ass." She glanced around the table as she straightened her spine before standing from her chair and taking a few steps back. Once in full view of everyone, she grasped the bottom of her shirt for a second before moving to the button of her pants.

"I told you it wouldn't work!" Autumn accused with a satisfied smirk.

"No. Take off the shirt, bellissima."

"But, the rules." She looked at Jensen as she wiggled and shimmied out of her pants, making sure her unrestrained breasts danced under her shirt, her hard, pebbled nipples guaranteeing the sway was noticed.

"You're tormenting me on purpose."

"Maybe, but I haven't broken any rules." She kicked her pants to the side of the room. "So, I win."

"Gwen, don't give him a reason."

Liv didn't get any further in her warning before Gwen dramatically rolled her eyes at her friend, a satisfied smirk on her face. She had won.

"The two of you practice the four D's right, Jensen?" Atticus' eyes never left Gwen.

"We do."

"Then, is there a reason your lovely sub *disrespectfully* rolled her eyes at me?"

"Wait, I didn't roll my eyes at you. I just," she sighed in defeat, "rolled them."

"Very disrespectful, bellissima." Jensen clicked his tongue against the back of his teeth. "What happens when you break the rules?"

Gwen crossed her arms over her chest. "You're enjoying this too much."

"Don't mumble, girl, I can't hear you."

Laughter filled the room. "You're supposed to be on my side."

Autumn shrugged. "We have been riding together in that ambulance for two years, and the whole time you played the sweet, little, innocent girl. Payback."

"I asked you a question. What happens when you break one of our rules?"

"I get spanked." Her eyes collided with his as she fought the smile that was trying to work its way to the surface.

"Don't count your winnings just yet. I'm about to wipe that triumphant look right off your face. The correct answer is you get punished. By me. In the way I choose. You will, more often than not, get spanked, but it is not the only punishment I have in my bag of tricks." He leaned into her and grasped her chin. "Not by a long shot."

She squirmed under his gaze. "But I was winning."

"You still are, but if you tease me any longer with what I am picturing is under that shirt of yours, I am going to embarrass myself. No pouting. Take the shirt off. Now. Quit looking at me like that, before I decide to give you a real punishment."

With a sigh, Gwen did as he bid. In one fell swoop, she tugged the shirt over her head and let it fall to the ground. How her nipples managed to pucker any further was beyond her. but they did, and the feeling had her rubbing her thighs together in an attempt to relieve the tingle.

Liv was the first one to talk. "They're so pretty. Can I touch them?"

Gwen didn't respond; instead, she turned to the man next to her with a quirked brow of her own. "What do you say, can she touch?"

"Fuck, yes," he groaned. "I still might embarrass myself."

The words were not even out of his mouth before she felt the chilled fingers lift her breast. She watched as Liv examined the bar that ran threw her areola. "And it didn't hurt?"

"Just the clamp," she whimpered as Liv twirled and pulled on the piercing. "I'm going to embarrass myself if you don't stop that."

Liv smiled over Gwen's head, the man behind her no doubt encouraging the other woman. "Like this?" She twisted the tip and the small bite of pain had her panting.

"No." Autumn climbed onto the table, on her belly, her naked ass exposed to the room. "Like this." She lifted the unclaimed breast to her mouth and gently suckled at the nipple as her tongue played with the bar.

"Fuck," Leland rumbled as he pulled Autumn from the table.

"Wait! I wasn't done playing yet."

"Hush now." As he tossed her over his shoulder, he nodded to the others as he strode from the room. "If you will excuse us."

Gwen watched as Liv stood from the table. "Atticus, will you walk me home? I think I started something that Jensen is going to have to finish."

"Hold on, lovie." Atticus closed his eyes and started mumbling.

"What are you doing?"

"Trying to get rid of this erection, so I can walk." After a few seconds, he opened his eyes, stood from the table and offered Liv a smile. "I'll get your coat. You find your clothes and meet me at the door. By then, I should be able to be the gentleman you need to escort you to your front door."

As soon as he left the room, Gwen called to the other woman, "Are you sure about this?"

"That I need to be walked home? No, but my husband made all his men promise to take care of me as he would if anything were to happen to him. I don't need half the department on my doorstep in the morning with their paddles in hand."

"I can walk you," Jensen offered.

"No, you take your girl home. It's only across the street. He will do the job just fine."

The women pulled on their few discarded articles, walked to the door and gave each other a hug. "Thanks for the game. I needed to get my mind off it for a while."

"The least I can do." Gwen ignored the sharp pain in her chest and the ever-present voice in her head as she watched the pair walk down the snowy gravel road.

"Gwen." She stepped into Jensen's arms and let him guide her to the truck. When she reached for the handle, he stopped her. "Are you all right?"

"Yeah, why do you ask?"

"Because you have been rubbing your chest like you're in pain and that smile isn't reaching your eyes."

"Just a little sad." She went to her toes and stole a kiss. "Because I get to do that without a thought and as often as I want. All she wants is one more kiss from him, and she is never going to get that." In an attempt to push the unchangeable away, she rubbed her groin against his jean covered thigh, reigniting the embers of lust.

He pinned her against the door and returned the favor, but his hard member hit home and the pressure on her sex had her knees going weak beneath her. He chuckled as he took a step away. "What is it with us and getting hot and heavy in the cold?"

"Please."

He just smiled as he gathered her in his arms, opened the door and boosted her into the truck. "I won't fuck you for the first time against the side of my truck. We need a warm, soft surface the first time." He slipped his hand between her legs, teasing her as he stole a heady kiss.

She whimpered when he pulled away. Once in his seat, he pushed the center console out of the way and pulled her to him. "Does that mean that after the first time, anywhere is fair game?" She moved to all fours and worked the button of his jeans as they reversed out of the drive and headed for his house.

His strangled groan had her smiling as she released his dick from his pants. "If our chances of getting arrested for indecent exposure are minimal." He sucked in a breath as she slid the crown of his cock into her mouth. "Don't you dare stop sucking, but don't make me come."

"How?"

He reached over and awkwardly popped her on the ass before tangling his hand in her hair. "I don't care how you do it, but if you make me come before I get inside of you, I will keep you on the brink of orgasm for as long as it takes me to be ready to go again. And if you stop before we pull into my garage, I will pull over and give you a proper spanking." Her groan had his hips bucking, sending his cock to the back of her throat. She wrapped her hand around his shaft as he settled back into his seat, pumping as she bobbed. "No hands, bellissima, I want you to take as much of me as possible. I want your mouth. Only your mouth."

She bobbed, licked and hummed against his cock the whole way back to his place. The few times he got close to an orgasm, he warned her with a tug to her hair and she was able to let up enough to hold him off. She was relieved when she heard his garage door close behind them.

With a tender pull of her hair, he drew her off his cock with a soft pop. "If you don't wipe that satisfied smirk off your face, I am going to have to take a leisurely drive around the block a few times."

Her smile widened for a second before she reached to take his cock into her mouth once more. The silky crest had just brushed her lips when he swung his door open and pulled her from the seat before tossing her over his shoulder. She squealed as his hand bounced off her ass. "Naughty little sub, thinking she can just suck me into that pretty little mouth of hers and I will forget who's in charge."

"Did it work?"

"Absolutely not." He kicked the door to the garage shut and walked the short distance to the house.

"Really?" She laughed as he entered the house. "I don't believe you."

"Why not?"

"Because you just walked the twenty yards between the house and garage with your stiff cock hanging out of your pants." She squealed as he tossed her on the bed.

"I meant to do that." Her snort was muffled by the fabric of his shirt as he whisked it over her head. When he pulled her bra from her body, he paused. "Really, baby?"

She looked down her body. "You don't like them?"

"I love them. I am just shocked that the whole time you were acting so innocent, you were hiding these beautifully adorned breasts from me. Naughty." He narrowed his eyes at her huffed laugh. "What else are you hiding from me?"

She shook her head. "I'm not telling you. You're going to have to find out for yourself."

He sucked one of her nipples into his mouth. "I have ways of making you talk."

While she was moaning, she watched as he pulled the previously untouched nipple into the hot recesses of his mouth. "They've been healed for years. Do your worst. Ow."

"Never taunt me when you have a body part so close to my teeth. I bite." The rest of her clothes were thrown to the floor in short order. Naked, sprawled across the bed, she watched him take inventory of her body. "No belly button ring. Stick out your tongue."

She did as she was told, laughing. "Wouldn't you have felt that while we were making out in the snow? Or against your truck?"

"You would think so, but I'm running out of places to search." He didn't get any further as realization dawned.

"By golly, I think he's got it." His eyes never left hers as his hand slowly ran down her body and over her naked mound. At his pause, she giggled. "Keep going, Sir, it won't bite."

The slow way he spread her lips drove her mad with need. When she arched into him, he drew his hand back and brought it down sharply over her pussy. "I'm not sure if that cry was one of pleasure or pain."

"Can it be both?"

"Hold your legs up with your hands behind your knees. I want to see your beautiful jewel." After a pause, a smirk split his face. "Both of them." She did as she was told. The cold air of the room on her hot, exposed sex only making her sexual need grow. "Keep making those little noises, baby. I love them."

He moved between her legs and the words fell from his mouth, "Fuck, baby."

"Do you like it?"

"Hell, yes." He took his cock in hand, stroking it from base to tip. "I should have let you make me come." She bucked off the bed when he shifted positions and ran his tongue over her sex, sucking her clit into his mouth and rapidly flicking the silver hoop imbedded in the hood of her clit back and forth with his tongue.

"I'm going to come," she cried out in anguish.

He released her tortured flesh. "You will not come without permission." Her whine was desperate. "All you have to do is ask nicely."

"Please, Sir."

"You can do better than that, girl."

"Please, please, please! Your mouth is so good and it has been so long, please, Sir."

"How long? As much as I love the beautiful blush of yours when it spreads across your face, it isn't going to keep you from having to answer my question. How long has it been?"

"Before I started at the station."

"Four years?"

Heat engulfed her clit once again. When he impatiently nipped the swollen bud, she cried out with the realization that he expected an answer. "Um, uh. At someone else's hand, yes."

"Good girl." He stood and shucked his pants. "Fuck, I should have let you suck me dry. Are you laughing at me?"

"Never, Sir."

"Lies, but I will let it slide because I love your laugh. It's infectious." He lay over the top of her. "It's going to be quick and hard, but I promise you, it will be good."

"Of that, I have no doubt." The head of his cock inching

into her had her arching into him. "Shove it in, please, Sir. Now, who's laughing at who?"

"I'm not a small man, Gwendolyn. I don't want to hurt you."

"And I'm not a virgin. You said hard and quick. That's what I want. Please."

"We will talk about you taking what you are given later. For now."

He drove into her, drawing another cry from her lips. "Fuck!"

"Fuck!" She wrapped her lags around his waist, hooking her feet together at the small of his back. She knew her heels were digging into him, but she didn't care; she needed the extra leverage.

He put his lips to her ears, nibbling the lobe. "If you don't stop trying to direct me on how to properly fuck you, I will pull out right now and paddle your ass. Then I will have no choice but to tie you down so you stop the manipulation." He chuckled. "You like the picture I put into your head?"

"Yes," she moaned as she reluctantly unwound her legs from him.

"Let's see if you like this." He rolled her to her side, straddled one leg, pinning it to the bed with his body. He pointed the other to the ceiling before he drove back into her, resting her leg on his chest and shoulder as he used her hip as leverage.

His thrusts were crazed, but he managed to hit the perfect spot every time, driving Gwen to the edge. "Sir. Jensen. Please."

"Say it. Tell me what you want."

"Please, Jensen. Make me come. Let me come."

"With pleasure." A slight tilt of his hips had Gwen throwing her head back and her internal muscles contracting in just a few strokes. "Squeeze me, bellissima, make me come. I want you to go with me. Now."

He rolled her clit firmly under his finger. Once, twice, on the third pass, she shattered. Her cry of pleasure was still bouncing off the walls as the roar of his release erupted from him. He thrust a few more times before he released her leg, fell to the bed beside her, and pulled her to his chest, dislodging himself from her body.

"That was." She searched for the right word.

"Embarrassingly fast?"

"No, I was going to say amazing, but I didn't want to stroke your ego any more than I already had." She settled her head on his chest, smiling at his feet. "Can we do that again?"

He rolled her onto her back, pinning her beneath his body, her arms above her head clasped in one of his hands. "Leave your hands there. Don't move them. Let's see how many times I can make you scream before our next round."

Chapter 12

"You would have thought your man hadn't seen you in a month, with the way he ran off with you last night."

Delight took over Autumn's face. "I know! We didn't even make it to the bed. He had me on my knees and his cock in my mouth as soon as he got the bedroom door shut."

"With the look on his face when you sucked my nipple into your mouth, I'm shocked he didn't take you from behind right there on the table."

"Trust me, I thought about it." Autumn smacked the arm that wrapped around her middle. "Meeting in the great room. PD is done with the personal devices."

"Did they discover that the arsonist is among us?" Gwen rolled her eyes as she fell in step beside the couple.

"Considering that no one was dragged off in handcuffs, I am going to guess no."

"Nice of the three of you to join us."

"How mad do you think Jensen will be if I flip off Starling right now?"

"Oh, I'll do it if you do!"

"No, you won't. The two of you will behave and not stoop to

his level." Jensen's hand rested on her lower back, leading her to a vacant chair. His mouth at her ear; he spoke only for her. "Behave, bellissima."

"Now that everyone is here, we found some interesting things on some of the computers." Starling's eyes shot to Gwen before skirting to a few other people in the room. "But we didn't find anything on the personal devices that infiltrated any of the users in the stalking of Miss Boisy or as the arsonist."

"So, you're going to move on and look elsewhere?"

"There is still someone using your IP address; we can't just ignore that."

"But, you just said we were clear." Jensen stiffened at her side as the argument fell from her mouth.

"No, I said your volunteered devices were clear."

"Just give us our stuff back."

Starling waved his hand toward the tables covered in tablets, phones, and computers, his gesture smug.

After working their way to the front of the room, he grabbed Gwen's wrist as she reached for her laptop. "I found your computer to be the most interesting."

She pulled her arm from his grasp and she tried again, but Starling beat her to it, swiping the device from the table. "I read them."

She paled the slightest bit, knowing it wasn't an accident that Jensen's things were at the other end of the long line of tables. She stood her ground. "Give me my laptop, please."

"You intrigue me, Miss Carlson."

"Laptop."

A sneer split his rounded face. "You play this innocent, homely woman at work, but your choice of reading material completely contradicts that."

"They are fiction, not autobiographies."

"Which is it? The frumpy, woman who hides behind the

men's clothes and a man's job? Or the sex crazed submissive, begging to be controlled."

She felt the heat rise in her face before she straightened her spine and looked the annoying man in the eye just as Jensen made it to her side. "That's sexual harassment, and I will be filing a complaint." As she snagged the laptop from the arrogant asshole, she spun on her heels, grabbed Jensen's hand and stomped away.

"You want to tell me what that was about?"

While dragging the man behind her, she marched into his office and collapsed into one of the chairs in front of his desk. "I cannot believe that infuriating, sexist man still has a job!"

"Gwen, I can't help you unless you tell me what happened."

"I can't, not while he's still in the building."

"Why not?" He snagged her around the waist, pulling her from her seat and into his lap as he took her place.

"Because I don't want to have to bail you out of jail."

"Oh, my God!" Autumn stormed into the office with Lee hot on her heals. "Did he really call you a frumpy, sex crazed submissive."

Gwen's head collided with Jensen's chest. "Not exactly."

"What?" Jensen roared as he went to his feet.

"No!" She wrapped her arms and legs around the big man and clung to him. "Jensen. You can't lose your head."

"The fuck I can't."

"Please, Jensen, just let me file a report with HR."

"Someone has to teach that asshole some manners."

"Sir, please." She wasn't sure what got through to him, the tear that slipped down her cheek or the use of his title, but she didn't care. For the first time since Autumn had opened her big mouth, he was actually looking at her and seeing her. "Please, just let me file a report with human resources. If you go out there like this, it's going to make it that much harder for me to get HR to take me seriously."

It took a couple of deep breaths, but after a few moments, he finally relented. "Okay, but you're not to be anywhere near him without someone else around if he is willing to say shit like that in a room full of people." A shiver ran through his body. "It terrifies me to think what he would do without the witnesses. Am I clear?"

"Yes, Sir."

"I really thought Jensen's head was going to explode."

"I thought I was finally going to get to see someone put Starling in his place."

"You couldn't have kept it to yourself for five seconds. All I wanted to do was file a report with HR, not have to talk my boyfriend out of decking a detective in the face."

"But it was amazing!"

As she shoved the door wide, she looked back at the girls. "Clinging to a man about to lose his shit and begging him not to beat the fuck out of a man you hate just as much as he does, is not my definition of amazing."

Ignoring her friend's glare, Autumn shivered as she pushed the door shut behind them. "It doesn't matter how many times I come in here, I still get goose bumps."

Kennly snorted. "Behave yourself, and you wouldn't be conditioned to dread it so much."

"Nah. Not going to happen. I think this is as well behaved as I get." With a shrug, Autumn led the way to the back of the room before she turned to the others. "We don't have much time before the guys come looking for us. What did you find out?"

All eyes swung to Kennly. "According to my dad, he is living with his mom in the same house he grew up in."

"I know where that is!"

"Hold it, turbo," Kennly said as she snagged the other woman by the arm when she tried to walk by.

"What? We have his info; we just need to ask him."

"We're on shift. I don't think pulling up to his house in an ambulance will give us the discretion this whole plot of yours requires."

She had the grace to look sheepish. "Okay, then tomorrow."

"Nope, I have another date with Jensen," Gwen said.

"Then it will just be Kennly and me."

It was Kennly's turn to disagree. "No, that isn't what we agreed. All of us, or none of us."

"We're not the fucking three musketeers."

"We are, or I walk out that door right now and rat us out." Gwen turned with every intention of doing just that.

"Fine! I-I just. Fine. When can we go?"

"I am free the day after tomorrow. Kennly?"

"I am free after five."

"I'll pick you up at three."

"Where are we going?" Each woman looked guiltily in the direction of the intruder. "The three of you are hiding something. It's written all over your faces. What's going on?"

"We're talking about something," Autumn stated, her poker face only slightly better than Gwen's."

"What?"

"Sex."

"Piercings."

"It is really none of your business," Kennly stated as she popped her hand on her hip.

After getting a different answer from each of the women, he turned to his girlfriend. "Autumn?"

"It's a surprise. I can't tell you about it. Not until I decide if I am really going to do it or not."

"Okay." The sound of the heavy door closing behind him had all the women breathing a sigh of relief.

"That was too easy."

"He didn't believe us for a second."

"How much do you think he heard?"

Gwen watched Autumn pace the length of the room. "I don't know, but if you are that worried about him finding out, then we really shouldn't be doing this."

"I'm not worried about him finding out. I have every intention of telling him. As soon as we have reached the point of no return. Any sooner than that and all this will be for nothing. I cannot go back to sitting on my thumbs."

"We'll be lucky if we'll be able to sit at all."

"You're not helping." Gwen turned to Autumn. "Calm down. Even if he did hear everything, we didn't say anything that could incriminate us."

"You threatened to rat us out! What reason would you have to do that if we weren't doing something dangerous?"

"We both know they won't jump to any conclusions without all the facts, so until they are able to connect all the dots, we're in the clear." Gwen watched her friend as she visibly relaxed.

"But they are absolutely going to corner each of us in an attempt to get us to spill. What? You can't tell me you actually believed they were just going to let us go about our merry way?" The expression on Kennly's face easily conveyed how dense she believed them to be.

"No, you're right, but Leland showed us his hand. We know it's coming."

"Which means the element of surprise is gone."

Gwen looked back and forth between the other women. "Whatever you do, don't lie."

"No, that would just make everything worse."

Gwen felt the tension leave her body. "Just tell the truth." She held up her hand. "We aren't in any danger, and the second we think we are, we will go to them."

"Will they accept that?"

"I don't know, but I made a promise and I intend to stick with that promise."

"When can we expect the questioning to start?"

"Soon."

"It was the cliché of fuckings. The bed bounced against the wall—the cries of passion, the slapping of skin against skin, but, fuck, it was hot."

"So?"

"So, what?

"How many times did he make you come before your next round?"

"Twice."

"My little Gwenny is growing up!"

"I've had sex before."

"I know, but you were my straight and narrow, vanilla partner for a long time. It's like my little baby bird is finally leaving the nest."

"And you're watching me plummet toward the ground?"

Autumn scuffed. "I'm just the mama bird. It's your Dom's job to catch you now."

Leland chuckled as he wrapped his arms around his girl. "That analogy is a bit of a stretch, princess."

"It got the job done." She looked into the man's eyes. "Is this the part in the day where you drag me off to unknown places and question me about our secret girls' meeting?"

"If you don't check that tongue of yours, this is going to be the part of the day where you get your ass smacked, repeatedly and vigorously."

"How about we do other vigorous activities instead?" Leland snorted as he led her away.

Gwen watched the couple leave the bay before she slammed

the doors to the rig, deciding to get her own interrogation over with. When the search for Jensen came up empty, she went to his office and sat behind the massive desk. A smirk playing on her lips as she cracked the top drawer open. When nothing jumped out at her, she opened it the rest of the way—pens, paper, the typical desk items.

"What are you doing in here?" Jensen questioned as he stepped through the door. When his eyes fell to the open drawer, the corners of his lips tugged up. "The stuff you're looking for is in the last one on the left."

She eyed the drawer in question. "What, exactly, am I looking for?"

"A way to distract me from getting to the bottom of what you girls are up to."

"Figured you were going to corner me eventually, so I thought I would make it easier for you." She propped her feet on to the massive piece of oak, determined to enjoy her illusion of power while it lasted.

She watched as he silently flipped the lock on his door before stalking to her, a squeal escaping when he plucked her out of his chair, only to settle her in front of him on the desk as he took his seat. As he opened the bottom left drawer just an inch, he continued his line of questioning. "Why would I need to corner you?"

"Leland walked in on the conversation the girls and I were having. He's talking to Autumn now. I figured we might as well get it out of the way." He rolled his chair closer to the desk. "Babe, I can't spread my legs any further in these canvas pants."

The corner of his mouth tipped as he opened the drawer another couple of inches. "Are you going to tell me what the three of you are up to?"

She locked her eyes on his. "I want to. I really do, but I can't." He played with the button of her pants before effortlessly popping it open. "But I can promise that if I believe we are in over our heads at any time, I will call you."

"Okay." He pulled her zipper down, exposing the edge of her panties. Running his finger under the band had his callouses catching the delicate lace.

"Really?" She saw the drawer, fully open now, and gasped.

"Yeah, bellissima, really. I trust you." The corner of his mouth hitched. "Now, I can't guarantee you won't get your ass paddled when I find out what you're hiding." He ran his finger over the newly exposed paddle. "But if you can tell me that you're not in any danger, I will let it go. For now." He pushed the implement aside.

"I went into this knowing I would possibly feel your displeasure when this was all over, so I will take whatever you decide to give me." She watched him pick up the tweezer clamps. "I really don't think we are in any danger, Sir."

"Okay, but I will keep digging." He popped the buttons on her shirt, spreading the fabric wide to reveal her bra. "They match."

Warmth spread across her face as he pulled her from her perch, shimmying her pants past her ass and down her legs. She smiled as she stepped out of the ring of fabric. "Of course." He quirked a brow at her double answer.

His hands glided over her soft thighs before cupping her ass, the rough handling causing her to squirm. She reached behind, unhooking her bra with a practiced ease as she rubbed her lace covered mound against his thigh and allowed her giggle to escape. "If you're not careful, you're going to end up with a zipper indentation permanently imprinted on your dick."

"On to the desk. Lie back and spread those thighs for me. Good girl." He plucked at her nipples, all but forcing her to arch into him, searching for more pleasure. When his mouth engulfed her pebbled tip, a cry fell from her lips. "Do I need to gag you?"

"No, Sir. I can be quiet."

"Good." He took the other peak into the warm cavern of his mouth, flicking the bar with his tongue. She whined when he released the flesh. "Breathe through the pain."

The words barely registered before she felt the pinch of the clamp as it took hold. "Fuck."

He gave her neglected nipple a flick in retribution. "Language." She sucked in a ragged breath as his clamp took hold of the other breast. Before the sharp bite subsided, she felt his knuckle graze her sensitive bundle as he pulled her panties to the side.

Buzzing hit her ears seconds before it hit her clit, the shock of it causing her to jump.

"Hand." He guided her digits to the bullet. "Don't let it move. Come when you can, but do so quietly." Her shiver ran the length of her body, the possibility of getting caught heightening her arousal.

She watched as he fumbled in his haste to get his pants undone. When his cock finally sprang free, he wasted no time in feeding it to her in one solid thrust.

The sudden invasion combined with the continuous vibration had her arching in pleasure as her first orgasm took over. His lips covered hers, swallowing her cries.

All it took was a slight shift in the direction of the vibrator and a dozen more thrusts before it was her turn to swallow his roar. As they caught their breaths, a smile spread across her face. "That was amazing."

"That was quick. I intended for it to last longer, but fuck, the vibration hit my dick and I was done for."

A shiver ran down her body. "Do you think anyone heard us?"

"Oh yeah, baby, they heard you."

Chapter 13

"Where are we going?" Gwen watched the trees pass as they wound their way up the hills, the headlights casting an eerie glow.

"Gwendolyn." The single word was growled in warning.

"But."

"I told you it was a surprise."

"But."

"And now I am telling you that if you ask again, I am going to pull this car over and spank that beautiful ass of yours." A huffed laugh passed his lips. "Your pout is doing nothing to convince me that I don't need to do just that."

She sat silently for a few more minutes before they turned and thousands of twinkling white lights came into view as the car came to the top of a hill. "This guy puts up these lights every year and has them up from November until the snow melts."

"It's stunning." Acres of trees were lit with the sparkling lights while the open spaces were canopied with the same artful swath. Benches and beautiful tables were scattered randomly under the lights. "It must cost a fortune."

"He lost his wife shortly after they were married. This is his way of remembering her." Gwen turned to him as he parked the car. "We're here."

"Here?"

"Yeah. I figured since we had so much fun with the snowball fight, I would tempt you with a picnic in the snow."

"Is it warm enough?"

"It's thirty-eight degrees. What do you say?"

The excitement that shone through in his eyes was all the encouragement she needed. "Can I pick where we have the picnic?"

"As long as it's well lit, I'll follow your lead."

Twenty minutes later, they were lying on a thick, wool blanket, another draped over them in the middle of the sea of lights. "This place is beautiful."

"I thought you would like it. Make a wish."

"A wish?"

"Yeah. People call this place *The Land of a Thousand Stars*, so it's only right that you make a wish."

She turned her face to his. "What if I can't think of a wish? What if I like things just the way they are?"

When he rolled toward her, he took her in his arms. "Flattery will get you anything you want, bellissima."

"In that case, I would kill for some of that hot cocoa." A squeal passed her lips as he pinned her to the blanket, her hands above her head.

"You only want me for my cocoa."

"No, but I figured since we were in a public place, I couldn't ask for the other."

"Cocoa and cock. I see how it is." As he placed both her hands in one of his, his other migrated down over her chest, stopping at her ribs as an evil smirk took over his face.

"Jensen?"

His face fell as a laugh erupted from her chest. "First, we're sucking face at the end of their driveway; now, you have me pinned under you in the middle of a public place."

With a pained groan, Jensen rolled onto his back, his arm thrown over his eyes. "Kill me now."

Gwen sat up and smiled at the couple. "Mr. and Mrs. Keetes."

"Greg and Daniella, please. What brings the two of you out here?"

Gwen giggled as she looked to their son. "Jensen brought me out here as a surprise." She turned back to the other couple. "But this surprise is way better."

He gave her a look full of the retribution to come before he sat up and addressed his parents. "Spread out your blanket and stay a while. I have a thermos full of spiked cocoa."

"We are actually on our way back to the car."

"Just decided to take a detour to embarrass your spawn, huh?"

Daniella crouched next to her son, her hand resting on her shoulder. "Get over it, sweet boy, you have nothing to be embarrassed about. So, your parents have caught you and your girl engaged in various stages of sexual activity; you are an adult. It happens." She shot Gwen a wink, and the older woman stood and spread out the blanket she held. "I guess one cup won't hurt anyone."

"Jensen, I can't tell if your mom just praised you or scolded you."

He smiled and handed a tin cup to his dad. "She's good at that, to this day. I still couldn't tell you if she was happy about me playing football in high school of not."

"Hated it," his parents announced in unison before it was his father's turn to tease his son. "Can't think of any date ideas that don't involve the poor girl freezing to death?"

Gwen said through her laughter, "In his defense, our first date started off in a restaurant, and the snowball fight in your back yard was all my doing."

"Laughing at my lack of imagination, bellissima?"

"No, I was just thinking how quickly I became comfortable with your parents and how not like mine they are. It's nice."

"Greg will have to take all the credit for that. My husband could talk to a brick wall and walk away with a friend." At her husband's snort, she continued. "You could! Prime example, Gerald Bass. He came over the other night. Do you remember how the two of you became friends?"

"We have been friends forever."

"No. His daughter, Baylor, got into a fight with one of our girls. He came over to see how you were going to deal with it, and thirty minutes later the two of you were sitting on the deck drinking a beer."

"Why does that last name sound familiar?"

"It's Kennly's last name. Must be her uncle or something."

"No, all his family is back in Washington State. He, his wife, and their three girls are the only Bass family around here."

"Is he a cop?"

"Yeah, retires next year. His oldest daughter, Baylor, followed in his footsteps and became a cop in some big city. Rumor was she was coming back home."

"Gwen, are you okay? You look like you've seen a ghost."

"I, um. Sorry, I was just wondering if he was Kennly's dad."

"I can only ever remember the one girl's name, but I know he said at one point that one of his girls was looking to be a firefighter. Maybe she finally got in."

"Must have, Kennly told me just the other day that her father was with PD."

"Too many coincidences for it not to be her. I'll have to give him hell for not sharing the good news."

"All right, husband, I am officially cold. Take me home."

"Demanding wench."

As soon as his parents were out of sight, Jensen flopped back on the blanket and gathered Gwen in his arms with her head resting on his chest. His hand rubbed slowly down her back before he sharply pinched her ass. "A sub making fun of her Dom. Whoever heard such a thing?"

"Ouch!" Their laughter echoed around them.

"I love this place. My parents used to bring us here all the time growing up." At her shocked expression, he laughed. "I didn't know the two of them came up here on their own. I swear."

Her teeth nipped at his rough jawline. "You really should stop stealing your dad's tricks of the trade."

He smiled down at her before turning his face back to the covering of lights. "I will bring you up here every year for as long as you'll let me. This will be our place."

"Our place."

Chapter 14

"Are you ready to tell me what you're keeping from me?"

Gwen smiled. "I think I want to keep you guessing, Sir."

Even over the phone, his chuckle sent a shiver down her spine. "I already know what it is, bellissima."

The goofy smile from only a second ago slipped. "How?"

"A man has his ways. I told you the other day that I would keep digging."

"And I said I was ready to face the consequences when you found something."

"It just so happens, we stumbled upon a clue last night."

"Your dad."

"Yeah."

"It was Kennly's dad."

"Yeah. It's not too late. The three of you could come home now, and we could forget all of this."

She looked around the quiet neighborhood, to the house they were approaching. "I can't do that, Sir."

The heavy sigh mingled with another chuckle. "All right, baby. Be safe."

"I will, promise."

Autumn spoke from the passenger seat as soon as she ended the call. "Do you think he knows?"

"He knows. We ran into his parents last night. Turns out, his dad is really good friends with Kennly's dad. It took off from there."

"What?"

As she turned in her seat, Gwen met Kennly's eyes, and she saw an emotion she couldn't quite put her finger on filling the depths. "Yeah, turns out your dad and Jensen's dad have been friends for years."

A harsh laugh escaped the other woman. "Really, how did I not know that?"

As she joined the conversation, Autumn stated, "If he knows, then so does Lee.

"And Zander." Gwen's mouth dropped open. "Oh, don't act so surprised. You saw him go all macho after Starling put his hands on me."

"But you never said."

"We are taking it slow," Kennly said.

"So, you haven't?"

"No, we have. We are taking everything else slow."

"Has he?"

"Okay, so the only thing we're taking slow is telling people about our relationship. Everything else, we did pretty quickly."

The laughter died as she pulled to the curb. The neighborhood was starting to get dark, the sun dipping behind houses as a small group of kids flooded into the street a few doors down, their laughter clear for the whole neighborhood to hear.

The house they parked in front of was bright yellow with a picket fence surrounding the front yard. "He lives here?"

"Yep," Kennly confirmed. "According to my research, he

grew up here. When he was released from prison, he came home to dear old mom and has been here ever since."

"It looks so normal."

Kennly snorted. "Autumn, what did you expect it to look like?"

"I don't know. Run down, shitty, maybe a few bullet holes. Not like this."

Gwen looked between the women she shared the car with. "I'm not sure about this. Jensen said it wasn't too late, and we could go back to the house. Forget all of this. Tell the cops how good he is with computers and let them decide if they want his help or not."

"Are you kidding?" For the first time, Autumn turned away from her window. "We already talked about this. We decided this was the best option."

"Yeah, but that was before. The guys know now; they can help us, and we can save our asses. Not only that, how exactly are we going to get the information to the cops, if we get any? We can't just walk up and hand it to them. What we're doing is illegal. It's a crime."

"But we are trying to help."

"It doesn't matter."

"Guys," Kennly's call from the back seat was ignored.

"It is still a crime, Autumn! Starling will arrest us so fast, our heads will spin."

"Then we don't take the information to him. We find someone else. We'll give it to Atticus, he's invested in this now. He'll help."

"Guys, he's coming."

"Who is?"

"Holy fuck!" Autumn screamed as a man's knuckles bounced off her window.

There was a tall, thin but muscular man with black hair and

dark eyes standing outside the car. Gwen swallowed nervously. He was pissed.

"Roll down the window."

"What are you doing?" Autumn's window continued it's decent. "Stop!"

"Gwen, we've come this far, we're not turning back now. We're here, he's here, we may as well talk to him."

"At least you have the decency to look a little sheepish, Autumn." He looked around the car. "Gwen, Kennly, nice to be able to put a face to the names."

Gwen narrowed her eyes at the man. "How do you know our names?"

"Well, I dated Autumn once, not that I would recognize her on the street now, but the three guys who showed up at my door this morning were nice enough to tell me the names of the women who would be visiting me today." All the women groaned at the same time. "They said that would be your reaction when I mentioned they had already been here."

"We're so fucked," Kennly whispered from the back seat.

"Did they tell you why we were coming?"

"They did." He looked around the neighborhood before handing her a small file. "This is all the information I could dig up. I tracked the IPs as best as I could, but I'm afraid they are still not going to be of any help to you. This guy is good. Every time I got close, he disconnected, and I lost it. I was able to narrow it down to some place in Hill City, but that was all."

Gwen stared at the papers as defeat settled into her bones. All this and they were still no closer to knowing who the arsonist was. "Thanks, Colt," she managed as she shifted the car into gear. The sooner they faced the music, the better.

"I will dig into it as often as I can, but I'm on probation. Not even supposed to have a computer in my house, let alone internet access, so it will be slow going."

"If you find something, you'll let us know?"

"No, those men of yours made it perfectly clear that any information I find goes to them." Autumn, throwing herself against the back of the seat, had Colt chuckling, "Yeah, he said you would react like that." He slapped the top of the car and took a step back. "Good bye, ladies. Have a good evening."

As soon as they pulled into Jensen's drive, the other women peeled off in different directions, leaving her there to deal with the none too pleased man standing in the open garage door with his arms crossed over his chest. "Chicken shits!" she yelled at them as they all but tripped over themselves to get to their cars before Jensen could lecture them. She straightened her spine then walked to Jensen and let him take her in his arms.

"Don't worry, bellissima, they won't get far."

"I don't doubt that." With her forehead resting on his chest, her words were muddled and muted. "How much trouble am I in?"

"Enough. Did you just growl at me?"

"No, Sir, just groaned. He didn't have anything for us."

"So, the three of you snuck around and kept things from us for nothing?"

Gwen turned to Zander as he joined them.

"Yeah."

Leland huffed a laugh as he took up his position on the other side of the couple. "Subbies."

"You're not just going to let them drive away, are you?"

"No, we disabled their cars." At her look of shock, he explained. "Simply loosened a battery cable."

She pulled out of Jensen's arms, looking into his dark eyes. "Can we get it over with, Sir?"

He took her hand and led her into the house and straight to his room. He shut the door before sitting on the bed and pulling her onto his lap. "Right now, the only thing I care about is why you didn't come to me. I gave you plenty of opportunities to do just that. The guys and I would have helped. You wouldn't have had to sneak around, and Colt could have started searching for information weeks ago. Now, you're facing a punishment that could have easily been avoided, had you only trusted me."

"I do trust you!"

"Then, why?"

A long, suffering sigh passed her lips. "At first, it was just an idea Autumn had. I didn't think it would go anywhere when we first talked about it. Then Kennly had all the information we needed, thanks to her dad, and next thing I know, we're pulling up in front of his house."

He pulled her head to rest on his chest, forcing her to breathe in his fresh, soapy scent with just a hint of the smoke smell he never quite got rid of. "The three of you are in so much trouble."

"I know, Sir." She eyed the paddle lying next to his thigh. "That's for me."

"It is." She shifted uneasily, as if it had already been used. "You will be fine, bellissima. Your ass will hurt, but you'll survive."

"I know." She forced herself to relax and bask in the feel of his arms wrapped around her, the feel of his warm breath rustling her hair—safe, loved.

They sat there for a few minutes before they heard a door in another part of the house slam shut. "Let's get this over with?"

She shivered as she stood from his lap. "Yes, Sir."

"Take off your pants and panties, then bend over the bed."

She worked quickly to do as he said, kicking the clothes to the side as soon as they pooled at her feet. With a deep breath, she took up the required position. "Spread your legs. I want to see that beautiful, glistening pussy." She groaned, his words creating more of the wetness he was referring to. "Spread your checks."

The three words had her head snapping up. "Sir?"

"Get back into position and do as you're told. If you make me repeat myself, I will add to what I'm already going to give you."

She swallowed hard, already knowing what was to come. With her head resting on the comforter, she reached back and pulled her ass cheeks apart, exposing her darkest secrets. "This is harder to do than I thought it would be."

"How so?"

"It's embarrassing and hot at the same time, but it's also a physically awkward position to hold." The cold dribble on her anus had her jumping and her hold slipping. "See what I mean, Sir?"

"Don't worry; you won't need to hold it for long." He worked the lube with his finger, making sure to coat her both inside and out. When he slipped the finger into her tight rosebud, a whimper fell from her lips. With each movement, he pushed it further into her, until her whimpers had morphed into moans.

"Ever worn a plug before?"

"Yes, Sir."

"How long?"

"An hour or so." She moaned, letting her eyes drift shut, hating how his playing with her ass made her feel so good.

"You will have this one in all evening." She looked over her shoulder. "Eyes forward. Good girl. You will also be expected to do things as you normally would."

"Sir?"

"That means no standing all night while we watch TV or eat dinner. You will sit as you normally would, paddled ass, plug, and all."

A surprised cry passed her lips as his warm finger was replaced by the cool of the metal plug. The joy he took in torturing her was evident. He pushed it in a bit before pulling it out, only to repeat the process. Her plea fell from her lips without thought. "Sir."

His weight settled onto her back as the fingers of his free hand honed in on her clit, alternating between taps, rapid flicks and pinches. "You're dripping. Do you like me playing with your ass?" A whimper was the only response she could muster.

He buried two of his digits in her core, the sudden invasion causing her muscles to flex around the pumping invaders. "Sir, I-I need."

"Don't you dare." He continued her torment with the plug but stilled within her pussy. "You do not have permission to come, and you won't." He chuckled at her cry of disappointment. "Girls who misbehave do not get rewarded." With the last word, he popped the plug into place. "God, I want you."

"Yes, please."

He chuckled. "Don't you want to know the conditions?" At her nod, he continued. "You're still not allowed to come. This would be solely for my pleasure. If you come, I will repeat your paddling."

It took a nip to her thigh for her to realize that he expected an answer. "Yes, Sir."

"Paddle first. I want to feel your hot ass against me as I thrust into you." She watched him pick up the paddle and spin it in his hand a few times. "Do you like our new toy? Zander bought it for us, just for this punishment." She groaned at his declaration. "Yeah, he says that's how Kennly reacts every time he pulls it out, too. Five."

She looked back at him, shocked. "That's it?"

"They aren't going to be love taps, but, yes, only five." The first swat had her arching her back and a curse falling from her lips. "Five is plenty." His next assault landed directly below the first. "Three more."

He didn't give her time to think, laying them down rapidly. The final swat landed across both of her sit spots, forcing her forward onto her belly as a sob fell from her lips. The sound of his zipper had her scrambling back into position. "Jensen."

"I'm going to fuck you, Gwen."

"Please."

She groaned as the head of his cock bumped her entrance. "Ask for it."

"Please fuck me. Please, Sir." In one solid thrust, he was buried to the hilt. "Fuck!"

"Fuck is right." His thrusts were almost brutal, but she loved it.

"Sir!"

"Don't you dare." He took hold of her hips, making sure to hit the spot he knew would drive her to the edge.

"I'm close. I can't hold it."

"You will!"

He pinched her clit hard before giving the ring embedded in her nipple a sharp tug, moves she would realize later were an attempt to help her hold off. "That's it, baby. Squeeze my dick." She did just that, and after a few thrusts, he buried himself deep in her core and let out a pained groan.

Chapter 15

"That man's sweetness is going to rot the teeth right out of your head one of these days."

As she rolled her eyes, Gwen flipped on the turn signal and took the corner just a little too sharply. "Woops."

"Woops, my ass." The other woman pulled on her seatbelt in an attempt to get it to loosen up as she flipped the other woman the bird.

"Eventually you will learn not to tease me when I'm driving." Gwen shrugged before changing the subject. "Think this is his?"

Autumn turned to look out the window, the flashing lights of the fire truck in front of them creating a soft glow of red around her dark hair. "Yeah, the marshal got a letter the other night."

As she gripped the steering wheel tightly, she shook her head. "I don't get it."

"You know no one but the firebug ever understands why they do it."

"No, I don't understand why he is still sending letters?"

"It's his calling card."

"But why? He talked to us on a live video feed. Why go back to snail mail? It isn't guaranteed that it's going to get there when he wants it to or that it will arrive there at all. Then what? He wouldn't get the recognition he thinks he deserves. He's already warned us about following the rules." Gwen backed the rig in as they arrived on scene and leaned her head against the back of the seat. "Something is off." The relative silence of the ambulance allowed her mind to wander and a nagging thought to take root.

"Are you ladies going to hide in that bus all night, or are you going to grace us with your presence on this *active* fire scene."

Hand over her heart, Gwen glared at the man standing outside her window. "What the fuck, Starling!"

"In case you hadn't noticed, we have a building on fire here."

The door narrowly missed the arrogant man as she threw it open. "We just got here."

"And were getting ready to what? Take a nap?"

Toe to toe with the officer, she felt her control start to slip as Autumn came to her side. "You want to do my job? You go right ahead." When his only response was a narrowing of his eyes, she huffed a laugh. "That's what I thought. Get off our backs and give us time to do our job."

"Medics needed at the ladder truck."

The radio crackled as she pressed the button and brought the mic up to her lips. "10-4, on our way."

"About fucking time you did your job."

The mumbled dig had Gwen turning back to argue, but a determined Autumn stepped in front of her. "Someone needs us." With a final glare, she followed her partner.

No one was found at the truck. "Medic to radio with traffic." After a few minutes with no response, she tried again. "Medic to radio with traffic." With still no response, she switched to plan b. "Chief."

"Go ahead, Gwen."

"Patient at the ladder truck not found. Anyone know of an ETA or who requested us?"

"Negative. I'll find out."

With a sigh, she sat on the rough, grated chrome at the side of the truck. "An arsonist who is just not quite right and then ghosted by a patient. Perfect day."

"At least it can't get—"

"Don't say it!" Gwen clapped her hand over the other woman's mouth. "Saying that is almost as bad as saying the 'q' word."

As she pushed her hand away, Autumn rolled her eyes. "That is an old medic wives' tale. You're not going to magically have more calls just because someone says the word quiet and something is not going to happen as soon as you say that it couldn't get any worse."

"Firefighter Boisy to dispatch."

"Go ahead, Firefighter Boisy."

"We have a situation. I need PD to meet me at the ambulance."

"See!" Gwen jumped from her perch, snagged the trauma bag and ran back to the ambulance. As soon as the rig came into view, she stopped in her tracks.

The rig sat low to the ground, all four of its tires flat, but what caught her eye first was the bold black lettering adorning the once pristine vehicle. *Whore. Tramp. Slut.*

"Looks like the arsonist is back to his old tricks again." Starling's strut brought him to her side.

"Something's wrong."

"No shit, Carlson. We have a sick and twisted arsonist in our city."

"No, I mean something is off."

"Bullshit!"

"Let her talk," Atticus demanded as he and Jensen joined the small group. "Go ahead, lovie."

"The arsonist wouldn't do this."

"Bullshit! He has already done exactly this at one of his previous fires."

"No, he didn't." Gwen's glare cut to the ignorant officer before she turned back to his superior. "Yes, the arsonist has painted the ambulance before, but it was nothing like this. It was a poem."

Atticus nodded. "I remember, something about fire being brighter."

"Yes! And why would the arsonist go from demanding that you protect the women of the station to calling us whores?"

"This wasn't him."

"What? You agree with them? They are glorified boo-boo kissers! Fuck, the only reason they are here is—"

"Say it." The growl came from deep within Atticus's chest. "Please, for the love of God, say it! It would be all I need to take that badge from your chest." After a pause, he continued. "That's what I thought. While you didn't say enough for me to demand your badge, you spewed enough hate from your mouth for me to remove you from this case."

"You can't fucking do this!"

"I can."

"This is the closest we have ever been to this guy; you pull me off now, and we will never get him!"

"You're right, we won't." Atticus gestured between himself and Starling. "But we will." He tapped himself on the chest before throwing his arm out and turning to the swarm of officers, firefighters and pedestrians who had gathered. "This community deserves better than you half-assing your way through this investigation."

"Did you get a plug put in your ass, too?"

"Right after the ginger."

"No ginger for me," Gwen said as she scrubbed at the side of the rig, determined to rid the vehicle of the hatred. "But then again, I am still not allowed to orgasm, so maybe I would have rather had the ginger."

"Never used ginger before, I will have to do some research." As soon as her elbow connected with his abdomen, she was gathered in his arms. "You're lucky we have a meeting with PD, or I may just have to poke you back." She tensed within the circle of his arms.

"Did you tell them about Colt? They can't know he was involved until he has information, maybe not even then. We can't risk it."

"Relax, Autumn, we didn't tell them anything, and we won't until we all decide the time is right."

"Or, you know, when they arrest us and we all start turning on one another. Whichever comes first."

"Smart ass." He traced Gwen's lips with his finger, tickling them slightly. "I love it when you smile."

"Even when it's full of sass and dripping with sarcasm?"

"Even then." He took her mouth forcefully, giving her no choice but to open for his invading tongue.

The clearing of a throat had her tearing her lips from his. "I am shocked and appalled at the public display of affection."

"Really? Because I seem to remember your eyes being glued to my mouth when I had Gwen's nipple in it during our game of poker?" Autumn jumped when Leland's hand landed on her ass.

"And what a wonderful game it was, lovie," Atticus teased as he swung his arm over the other woman's shoulder.

"Get your own brat, Pardoe." Leland snatched his girl from under the man's arm.

Laughing, Atticus addressed the group. "Should we go to Jensen's office?"

As soon as the door was shut behind them, all humor was gone. "No one else can know about this meeting." When he got the affirmation he needed, Atticus continued. "We believe the copycat is someone close to the case; it's just a matter of narrowing it down at this point."

"Wait, so there's a copycat? I knew something was off!" Gwen looked around the room, catching the eyes of each person. "Why are Autumn and I the only ones shocked by this news?"

"We couldn't tell you."

Gwen veered back as if she had been slapped. "You guys already knew there was a copycat?"

As he swore under his breath, Jensen rubbed his hands across his face before looking the woman in the eye. "Yes, but we were not at liberty to share the information. I wanted to. God, did I want to." He rolled his head back, a move Gwen knew was an attempt to stay calm.

Too bad it didn't work for her. "You wanted to tell us? Would that line have worked for us when you guys found out about it?" Her eyes cut to Atticus. "Would it have worked the other night? Would it have kept us from getting out asses paddled or from being plugged?"

"Gwendolyn."

"Save your warning. I don't want it." She only got three steps toward the door before her wrist was clasped in an unrelenting grasp. Pissed, she spun on the culprit. "Let go."

"Hear us out." Her only response was an attempt to escape his hold. "If I would have told you, I would have been arrested. I wanted to tell you, but I couldn't."

While she pulled her arm from his grasp, she huffed a laugh. "I'm pretty sure I said something like that right before the cold lube hit my ass."

"This is different."

"Different? Please explain, because I am having a hard time seeing the difference."

"That's because all you're seeing right now is red." When his strong arms wrapped around her, she struggled. As she was contemplating the wisdom of kicking him in the shin, he said, "Be still, bellissima."

She hated how the softly spoken phrase had her fight melting away. A simple endearment and she was a goner. "You fight dirty."

"No, I just use every advantage at my disposal, and it just so happens that you're—"

"Madly in love with me," she finished the familiar phrase. With a sigh, she turned in his arms, burying her face in his chest. "This isn't an issue that can be fixed with a band aid. I'm angry and hurt, and I don't see the difference between our two situations, other than you're not going to get a paddle taken to your ass."

A kissed landed on the crown of her head. "I couldn't tell you. Atticus made it perfectly clear that if word of the copycat got out, it would end with us in jail."

"I feel like I am missing something." Gwen let her eyes drop to the floor, afraid Atticus would read their secret in her eyes.

"You three chose to keep something from us because you didn't trust us to help you without taking over or hearing you out." It was Autumn's turn to be gathered in her man's arms

"You did take over. Ow." Her hand fell to her ass, rubbing the slight sting away.

"The direct communication with him, yes, but every choice that is and will be made is made together." When a response wasn't forthcoming, Jensen tipped her head up with a knuckle under her chin. "Do you see the difference now? My eyes are up here."

It took a few deep breaths, but Gwen was able to force her eyes to his, heat engulfing her face. "Yes, Sir, I understand. Just don't do it again."

"I promise, if I ever discover a copycat arsonist again, I will tell you."

"That's all I ask."

When the laughter finally died down, Jensen took a seat, pulling her into his lap before he turned to Atticus. "I think we are ready now."

"This copycat creates an entirely new level of danger. We can't leave the girls unprotected."

When all he received were nods of agreement, he continued. "I have made arrangements for the girls to have a ride along. He's an undercover cop, and he starts next shift."

Jensen looked around the room. "You didn't pull us in here just to tell us that. What is it?"

"Our IT guys have found something."

"What does that mean?"

The officer's eye shot to Leland for only a second, but it was enough to raise the other man's suspicions. "What is it?"

"They ran into a live feed."

"Like the video the arsonist sent to the station?"

"Not exactly."

"Quit being cryptic and just tell us what the hell is going on?"

"The feed was of Sierra's apartment. Real time."

The sound of Leland's fist going through the drywall had Gwen jumping to her feet. "Leland?"

"Fuck!" Leland shook his hand out to alleviate the pain. "Fuck!"

Jensen slowly rounded the chairs. "Boisy, lock it down."

"I'm good. I. My sister!"

"Lock it down."

"That's not it." When all eyes landed on him, Atticus continued. "It popped up so suddenly that I am pretty sure the guys were led to it."

"Meaning?"

"We believe that the original Hill City Arsonist led us to a feed that the copycat installed."

"Why?" Gwen watched as Leland gathered her partner in his arms and buried his nose in her hair.

"We don't think any of the recent 'arsonist' activity was the work of the original fire starter."

"Which means the copycat is the bigger threat, at this moment."

"Much bigger. It also means that someone close to the case is targeting you guys."

She felt the color drain from her face as a chill took over her body. "Do you think Sierra's house is the only place he has cameras?"

"We're not sure. She was the original reason we brought our guys in to your station, but this is beyond the computer hacking we thought it was." He looked to each person in the room. "We have men on standby, waiting for permission to search all of your places for cameras, including Liv and Kennly's."

"Do it."

As soon as the girls consented, Atticus pulled his phone from his pocket and left the room.

"Gwen?" His voice pulled her from the idle study of the island's countertop.

"I couldn't sleep."

"Have you slept at all?"

"No."

"Do I need to pull you off the rig?" Ignoring the question, she took a long pull from her mug, the warm liquid chasing away the chill she hadn't realized had settled over her. "I'm worried about you." He silently took the seat next to her.

"What if he's been in my apartment? I sleep there. That's where I dance in my underwear. Fuck, Jensen, I sing in the shower!" She knew she was being irrational, and those things should not be what she was worried about, but it was all she could think of. "I can't hold a tune to save my life."

"Gwen."

When he took her hand in his, she pulled away. "He violated my space. My home. Me!"

She squealed when she was pulled from her seat and settled on his lap, her face automatically going to his neck. "We don't know if there are cameras yet."

"You heard Atticus; there could be! What if there are? I can't go stay with my parents like Sierra did."

"If there are, then you will stay with me, but we don't know yet. There's no sense in borrowing trouble."

A sob rocked her body. "There are two of them, Jensen. Two people targeting our shift, our people. Our friends. I can't lose another person. I can't."

Chapter 16

"I told you the calls were boring," Gwen called to the back of the rig as they pulled into the bay.

"Do we go to all the arsonists' fires?"

"We go to all the fires. It's a precaution." She climbed from the rig and plugged the vehicle in before turning to their undercover agent. "The best part of these calls, we don't have to restock the rig."

"That was the arsonists', right?"

"Won't know for sure until the fire marshal comes in and inspects, but it sounds like it." Dread gnawed at her.

With a nod, he pulled a pack of cigarettes from his pocket and headed for the door. "Smoke break. Don't leave the building."

"Asshole."

"Tell us what you really think of him." Laughter echoed off the walls.

"What do you think of him?"

With a shrug, Autumn headed for the great room. "I don't know if I would trust him with a patient, but I guess that isn't why he's here."

"Thank God! I thought it was just me being difficult." Gwen slumped against the counter with a forced chuckle. "A patient would bleed out from a paper cut before he got the damn Band-Aid. I'll start the coffee."

"Don't want to deal with your man without buttering him up first?"

"Are you kidding?" Gwen questioned as she opened the cupboard. "I may have gotten a little short with him earlier so, yes, I am going to suck up as much as I can in order to save my ass."

When she turned back to her friend, her heart stopped. "Autumn, what's wrong?" She followed her line of sight to the TV mounted in the corner. On the previously black screen, was the same dark silhouette as before. With a few quick steps, she was at her friend's side, clutching her hand and pulling her phone from her pocket.

"Cell jammer, trying to call the guys will do no good."

The computerized voice sent chills down her spine as a nagging warning went off in the back of her head. She made a show of setting the phone on the counter.

"How did he know you were getting your phone?"

"The bugs."

"Now, girls, I am disappointed in you. Contrary to popular belief, planting bugs in places they have no business being is not one of my talents. However, I am going to use every avenue the copycat leaves for me, especially if it will help me keep you safe. I simply tapped into his feed; the rest was easy. I am a person of great capabilities."

"What do you want?"

"All I have ever asked from the Hill City FD is that you follow the rules. That, and the protection of you girls."

"How can they protect us when you are manipulating them by distracting them with the fires?"

"I haven't burnt since." The silhouette shook his head sadly.

"These recent fires have not been mine, but I think you already know that, don't you?" When neither woman replied, he continued. "I started all of this to protect you girls. You are the treasures of the department, and this imposter is putting that in jeopardy."

"Lies. You started this to feed your need to burn, like every other arsonist who has ever existed."

"You are wrong, and unfortunately, you will know that sooner, rather than later. You see, a rule was broken today."

"A rule?"

"The most important one. Your protection. As a direct result of this lapse in judgement, one of you was hurt."

"What did you do to Kennly?"

"Now, Gwen, I'm disappointed in you. I would never hurt you girls."

"What did you do to Kennly?" The demand was sharp, but she couldn't help it. Fear had settled into her gut and was threatening to take over.

"Kennly is fine, Gwendolyn. I didn't hurt her. I would never hurt any of you. But since she didn't follow the rules, Sierra got hurt by someone else.

"What did you do?"

"Nothing, but I have these rules in place for a reason."

"So you've said. Where is she?"

"She is on her way, but you need to prepare yourselves and know that I tried to get her out of there, away from that… *man*. I tried so hard, but there was only so much I could do. Her taxi should be arriving at the station in just a few minutes. I—" Gwen watched as something out of frame caught his attention. "Someone is outside the station."

"Our student ride along; he has a nasty habit."

"No, I am turning off the jammer. Call the police."

Autumn had her phone to her ear in a second. "Damn right, we have the fucking arsonist on a—"

At first, Gwen thought it was a firecracker, but the reality of the situation set in as Autumn's weight collided with her, knocking the breath from her chest and taking the two of them to the ground behind the island. "No, no, no, no, no!" Gwen frantically searched the other woman for wounds. "Damnit, Autumn. I cannot do this again!"

"I wasn't hit. I was just—"

"We don't have time. He's leaving!" Gone was the calm and collected man from before; in his place was a frantic and, was that worry? "The jammer's disabled. Call the cops before he gets away!"

Gwen picked up her phone and put in the necessary numbers before putting it on speaker and heading for the door.

"911, what's your emergency?"

"My name is Gwendolyn Carlson. I'm a paramedic at the Hill City Fire Department." She burst through the front door as a car peeled away from the curb, tires squealing in its wake. A yellow taxi pulled into the now vacant space. "We have shots fired outside the station. A dark SUV just left the scene. Send units."

"Ma'am, I need you to slow down. I—"

She took in the sight in front of her. A crying Sierra was gingerly climbing out of the taxi, but the wounded woman only held her attention for a second. It was the growing pool of dark, ugly red surrounding the crumpled form next to the building that had her dropping to her knees.

He was dead. The hole in his forehead made that sickeningly clear.

Chapter 17

The sound of the door opening had everyone on their feet. "How is she?"

"She's in pain, but she'll be fine." Autumn sighed heavily before dragging her eyes to meet his. "I need you to lock him down. She won't talk to anyone until she knows that Leland won't go off the handle."

Jensen didn't have to look behind him to know that Zander was right on his heels. One of their brothers needed them, and they were damn well going to be there for him.

He didn't know what he expected to see when they rounded the corner to Sierra's room, but it definitely was not the scene playing out in front of him. Kennly and Gwen stood side by side in the doorway, neither willing to give an inch and both giving the livid man standing before them a piece of their minds.

"Jensen, thank fuck, tell your sub to get out of my way."

"I can't do that, man." At the other man's roar of frustrations, he continued. "That's why."

"She's my sister. She needs me."

Liv walked out of the room, stepping up to Leland so they

were nose to nose. "You're right; your sister needs her brother. She needs her *strong, controlled, caring* brother."

"Then let me in!"

"You are not any of those things right now."

"A bear with a thorn in his paw." All eyes fell to the woman standing in the doorway behind Gwen and Kennly, her voice small and a bit pained.

"Or an older brother denied his baby sister." All the anger that had been rolling off the man a few seconds ago visibly simmered just below the surface.

Jensen stepped in front of his friend. "Take a walk. Go punch a wall, something. Take five minutes to get your shit together. We need to hear what she has to say, and she won't talk to anyone with you like this." With a quick nod of his head, Leland spun on his heels and walked away as he pulled his cell from his pocket.

"You were told to stay in bed."

"I'm fine." Sierra brushed off the concern with a wave of her hand.

"We don't know how the pain medication is going to affect you, and until we do, you are to stay in bed."

"You don't get to go all bossy with me, Liv."

"Actually, when you're my patient, I get to do exactly that." When Liv's eyes fell to him, Jensen moved to do her bidding, but he only got a few paces before he was cut off by Zander.

A small, startled cry passed Sierra's lips as she was swept off her feet. "Zander Allen, put me down."

"I don't take orders from you."

"And I don't take orders from you anymore, so put me down!"

"When I am twice your size and you've been admitted to the hospital, you don't have much of a choice."

Jensen had to turn away from the bickering pair to hide his smirk. In doing so, his eyes collided with Kennly's, her face unreadable.

"How are you feeling?"

"For the thousandth time, Liv, I feel fine."

"Liar." Leland walked right up to his sister, pushing Zander from her side.

He took the hint and walked back to Kennly, wrapping his arms around her middle as he sat in a chair and pulled her onto his lap, both content to sit on the sidelines.

"Just got off the phone with Dad. I told him you were fine and not to worry, but you had an accident and you won't be home tonight."

She flinched. "Lee, I—"

"You were supposed to be staying with them while your place was swept for bugs."

While she plucked at the necklace at her throat, she pleaded with her furious brother. "Please, Lee, you—"

"You lied. Dad thought you were staying with me." He turned away, his eyes catching Jensen's as he raked both hands through his hair and headed for the door. Without a word, Jensen followed the other man into the hall. "She lied, Keetes. She never lies. Damn it!"

The clattering of the chair as it bounced across the floor drew the attention of a few nurses. "He's fine." Jensen held up his hands, hoping to mollify the situation a little. "He's locking it down."

"She fucking lied." They walked into a small, empty waiting room at the end of the hall.

"Yeah, she lied, but that isn't what's important right now."

"Not important? For the last week, no one has known where she was, and then she rolls up to the station with a dislocated shoulder. That is pretty fucking important."

"What is yelling at her going to accomplish? Scolding her isn't going to get you the information you want. Acting like an asshole isn't going to get you anywhere but kicked out of her room and this hospital."

Jensen wasn't shocked when the fist connected with his face; he knew it was coming. If he were honest, he would admit he had been pushing for it. He swiped at the corner of his mouth with his thumb. "That's the only free shot you get."

"Good." He was able to duck before the next one landed, his own fist bouncing off the other man's stomach, forcing a satisfying grunt. He followed up by wrapping his arms around Leland's middle and taking him to the ground, colliding with a few chairs. "Are you done?"

"Not by a long shot."

He had the other man pinned to the ground for only a few seconds before he was pushed off and Lee was on his feet. Jensen slowly stood, knowing that as soon as he was on an even playing field with Leland, he was free game. The blow was enough to force the air momentarily from his lungs, the momentary shock giving Lee enough time to land another hit on the other side of his abdomen. Grunting, he swung at his friend. When the other man ducked, his fist missed its mark and made contact with the side of his face, seemingly knocking some sense into him.

Panting, Jensen slid down the wall and looked at the man lying on his back next to him. "Shit, man, if you wanted to fight, all you had to do was ask."

"You would have held back. I needed to go a few goods rounds, no holds barred."

"You needed your ass kicked." He eyed the other man. "You're going to have a black eye."

"It will go nicely with the split lip you're sporting."

"Feel better?"

He scuffed. "I'm still sending Dad after her, but I think she'll at least be able to get a word in edgewise now."

"Good." Jensen stood, straightening the disheveled furniture before he held his hand out to the other man. "Let's go talk to your sister."

"Tell me you didn't break anything." Liv stood in the hall with her arms crossed over her chest, foot tapping.

"Nurse Liv, I promise you, nothing was broken, just knocked him down a few pegs."

"I have to go do rounds; don't do anything stupid before I come back."

Sierra called to her brother as soon as they walked into the room. "Lee, I'm sorry."

"What am I going to do with you, Cici?" He climbed into her bed, carefully gathering her in his arms.

Her response was muffled by his chest. "Probably tell Dad."

"He already knows. You've got some explaining to do, little sister." He pulled her away from him and trapped her eyes with his own. "We need to know what happened."

"You going to go off the handle?"

"You going to tell me the truth?"

"Yes."

"Then, no."

She took a deep breath. "His name is Devon. I met him a couple of months ago. He's sweet and funny, always so careful with me when we play." She swallowed hard. "He's been taking a Shibari class for months now. He asked me if he could practice on me." When groans erupted in the room, her eyes dropped. "It was just a simple tie."

"You know better."

"I know, but I see him practicing all the time. He's careful, and it was just a corset with a simple arm restraint." A tear ran down her face.

"Go on."

"He checked on me as he was tying. It felt amazing. I don't know what happened. One second, I was standing, the next, I was on the ground in pain. He tried to catch me, but he wasn't fast enough."

"If it was an accident, then why isn't he here?"

"He wanted to come, but I begged him not to. I knew Liv was working and would know I was here as soon as I arrived. I didn't want that to be your first impression of him." Her eyes drifted to the left as she fingered her necklace.

Gwen grabbed his hand, giving it a squeeze. She had seen it, too. As he led her to the hall, his one word said all it needed to, "Bellissima."

As soon as his arms were wrapped around her, a sob escaped. "She's lying. If he was such a great, caring guy, then where is he? Where the hell is he?"

"You're right."

"It's more than that. He put her in a fucking cab, Jensen. A cab! Her shoulder was obviously dislocated; any fool could see that." She pushed on his chest, her anger building. "He didn't even call her an ambulance!"

"Something isn't right."

"It wasn't an accident!"

"I don't know if I would go that far, but it is definitely messed up." He let her silently cry into his chest, the sobs twisting his heart every time they shook her body. When she finally settled, he wrapped her hair around his fist, giving it a little tug so he could see her face. "Bellissima."

"I'm fine."

"You witnessed a murder."

"I'm fine!"

His hand bounced off her ass before he thought better of it. "That has never been an acceptable answer."

Her knees crumbled when the second swat landed and he sank to the floor with her wrapped in his arms—exactly where he needed her to be.

Chapter 18

The sound of voices had her lifting her head from Jensen's lap. "You don't have permission to move."

"I didn't know I needed it."

"You need it if I tell you that you do."

"There are people here." The pinch to her thigh had her adding a forced, "Sir," to her comment.

"So, be a good little subbie and let me hold you before I decide to spank your ass properly."

She gave in to the gentle pressure and laid her head down. "We can't sit on the floor forever, Jensen. The janitor has already had to mop around us once. Let me go."

"No."

"He isn't going to give an inch, lovie," Atticus said.

"What good will all this protection do if he smothers me?"

"You were within feet of a murderer, seconds after he killed a man. Jensen is allowed to smother you for a while." He sighed. "I am afraid the information I have is not going to change that any time soon."

Gwen rolled her eyes at the worn leather shoes in front of her. "He doesn't need any help from the peanut gallery. Ow."

"And Atticus doesn't deserve your sass."

She pushed her butt into his punishing hand, meaning the words that fell from her lips, "I'm sorry, Sir."

"How much worse can this be?"

"They completed the search of the girls' places. We didn't find any cameras or listening devices."

"Thank God. Then what's the problem?"

"We searched the station after Gwen told us about the video feed. We found multiple cameras, in nearly every room. The only good thing is that, from what we have found, the arsonist accessed them mere hours after they were put in and then disabled the cameras in the locker room."

A sob was torn from her chest as Jensen pulled her into his lap, her legs straddling his. She sat like that for a few minutes before she swiped at her face with the back of her hand. Then she turned to the man now crouching next to her and asked the only question that came to mind, "What does this mean?"

"It means our copycat has access to the station."

"And we're sure they are not one and the same?"

"We're sure."

"How sure?"

"We pulled a partial print from one of the bugs and have a sixteen-point match. We're close; we just need to wait for him to mess up."

"Go to sleep."

She rolled her eyes in the dark of the room. "I'm trying."

"Don't roll those beautiful eyes at me."

"How did you?" She stopped abruptly, realizing she was in the process of confessing. "You fight dirty."

"No, I use every advantage I have; it just so happens that you're madly in love with me."

Her snort was anything but ladylike. "You're not helping the whole sleep situation."

"Do you need help getting to sleep?"

"That depends."

"On?

"How you intend to help me."

"A fun way, of course."

"Fun for both of us?" He had her pinned to the bed before she quit talking.

He rubbed his thinly veiled cock against her thigh. "What do you think?" When her legs fell open, a triumphant smile spread across his face. "That's what I thought." A whine tumbled from her lips as he rolled off her. "Hush. I am just getting a few things, you know, to help you sleep." She watched him as he flipped on the light and gathered the items he wanted.

"What are you planning?"

"That is the beauty of being in charge. I don't have to tell you."

"Please."

"No."

"Just a hint?"

"A gag."

He returned and let his selections drop to the foot of the bed before he grabbed the rope and walked to her side. "Don't try hiding it, bellissima. I know you like what you see."

She knew excitement set her eyes aglow, but she didn't care in the slightest. She wanted him to know how hot he made her. "Not hiding a thing, Sir."

One swift tug had her shirt over her head and a groan rumbling from his chest. Her lace bra did nothing to hide the tantalizing, silver bars that ran through her nipples.

Never one to deny himself, he released the front clasp and pulled the offending garment from her body. As soon as it was out of the way, he took her pebbled tip into his mouth, sucking greedily before switching to the other.

Her moans filled the room, loving his lips on her. She ran her finger through his hair, earning herself a sharp nip as her tender flesh fell from his mouth.

"Slide down, so your arms can stretch out above your head." She did as she was told, smiling the slightest bit when his cock twitched behind his boxer briefs.

"You're not going to let me touch you?"

While he made quick work of it, he tied her wrist to the rings hidden behind the headboard. "You can touch me." He ran his fingers down her arm and over her ribs, causing her to wiggle under his touch. "Next time. Pouting will get you nowhere, my girl."

She pulled on the restraints. When they held, she relaxed and watched him grasp the waistband of her pants. "I could have stripped for you, and then you wouldn't be stuck doing all the work."

He shimmied her pants down her hips to her mid thighs. "This is anything but work, bellissima." One swift tug and her pants were gone. "I love the practical underwear you wear to work."

She groaned, "I never claimed them to be practical." As he looked down her body, he admired the pink thong and she added, "It makes me feel sexy, and I need all the sexy I can get when I'm stuck in the uniform for twenty-four hours at a time."

"We will have to make sure that *this*," he plucked at the thin strap encircling her waist, "remains our little secret."

She smiled at him, loving how he made her feel special in the simplest ways. "Our little secret."

"It's almost a shame to take them off. Almost." He slid them slowly down her legs and over her feet before he ran his eyes back up her legs.

"How is this fair? You're still in your boxers."

He shook his head teasingly. "You've forgotten who's in charge. Open."

Her eyes rounded as he balled her panties in his fist. "Um."

"We're playing, so tell me what your safeword is?"

"Labradoodle, Sir."

"Are you using it?"

Was she? She had been gagged before, but she had a feeling her panties were about to be pushed between her lips. The thought both thrilled and worried her, but excitement won out. "No, Sir."

He placed a rubber duck in her hand. "Squeeze it." She did as he told her, the obnoxious squeal making her giggle. "Open." She chewed on the inside of her lip for a second, but as soon as his brow rose, her jaw went slack. "Good girl." He thrust her wadded-up underwear into her mouth. "No more interruptions."

Her tongue played along the fabric, her spicy taste coating it. Fuck, her own flavor should not turn her on, but the taste of her essence forced her body to create more and when she rubbed her legs together, her muffled moan filled the room.

A sharp slap fell on her left thigh. "If you don't quit doing my job for me, I'll tie your legs, spread you wide, and torture you until you're begging through your gag to come."

Another moan, but she spread her legs for him. He was in charge.

"Beautiful." He ran a single finger up the inside of her leg before cupping her pussy. "And soaked."

She arched off the bed when two of his digits sank into her core. With each determined thrust, his palm rubbed her clit. "I love watching you, but when you're this close to the edge, it's impossible to take my eyes off of you."

She cried out when he pulled his fingers away and turned to the discarded items. When he turned back, he held a small, red crop. "You can claim as many orgasms as you want. You have my permission, just for tonight."

Instinctively, her legs snapped shut when the square of leather fell on her exposed core. Without a word, he dropped the implement, fastened cuffs around her ankles, looped some rope through the rings and spread her wide. "Let's try this again." The blows fell slowly at first, allowing her to get used to the feeling, but they quickly picked up speed.

She writhed and cried out, arching toward him after each strike. It hurt, but she wanted more. Needed it. One, two, three. The strikes kept coming. With the sixth, so did she. Screaming behind her gag, she convulsed with her release.

"Beautiful." She was panting, and she watched through half lidded eyes as he tossed the crop to the floor before plucking a rabbit vibrator from his stash and clicking it on. He ran the whirling toy over her primed sex, only allowing it to tickle her clit for a second before pulling it back. Again, and again, he taunted her.

Just as she was about to lose her mind, he buried the well lubricated phallus in her core. That was all it took to send her primed body into orbit again. When the clit tickler settled into place, the orgasms crashed into one another until all she felt was bliss.

She was floating.

The heat of his body as he settled over her drew her back to reality. "My beautiful girl." She wetted her lips as her panties were pulled from her mouth seconds before his hand found her wrists and he pinned them to the bed, taking away what little range of motion she had. "I need to hear you scream my name when you come on my cock. Can you do that, baby?"

"Please." That was all the encouragement he needed before he entered her. His strokes were tender. Meeting his thrust, she begged for more. "Please."

"My baby likes it hard?" A thrust of her hips was all the affirmation he needed before he pounded into her with short, rough thrusts. As he panted between words, he warned her, "I've tormented us long enough. Come for me." His head fell to her breast, sucking her nipple into his mouth and biting it sharply.

His name echoed off the walls as her release took hold. Her eyes rolled back as her body went rigid, her inner muscles clamping down on his invading cock.

"Fuck, Gwen!"

She felt him stiffen above her as she came down from her high, his own release taking over. His thrusts slowed as his head came to rest on her chest, their panting mingled together, his breath warming her skin.

Perfect.

A smile split her face as her eyes grew heavy and she realized the weight that sat on her chest had dissipated. This was exactly what she had needed. No control. No decisions to make. Just him and their trust and love for each other.

Perfect.

Chapter 19

"Why are we here?" Gwen looked down the line of women standing at her side.

"The firemen's ball is coming up. We need dresses."

"I don't think I'm ready for this." All eyes fell to Liv. "I-I don't think I can go without him."

"This year's ball is in his honor, Liv, you have to go."

"That is exactly why I can't. I don't want it to be in his honor! I want his arms wrapped around me as we twirl around the dance floor and for him to catch me a hundred different times when I trip over my dress." Tears leaked from her eyes.

"Okay," Gwen stopped the group as she turned to the weeping woman. "Then you don't go." She shrugged. "We stay home and eat ice cream, look at all the old pictures of the past firemen's balls and laugh at the ugly dresses we wore." She took her friend's hand in hers. "In the meantime, we get you a dress, different from any of the other ones you've worn before. Just in case you decide you want to go."

"You would really stay home with me?"

"Of course."

Liv shook her head in agreement as she rubbed away the tears. "I need a dress I won't trip over."

"Or a pantsuit; you could totally rock a pantsuit." It was Kennly's turn to have all the eyes on her. "What?"

"No!"

Gwen pulled back the curtain and stepped out of the fitting room.

"Blue? You do realize this is the Firemen's Ball, right?"

She looked down at the beautiful dress. "Yeah?"

"Fire is red. Blue is police. You wear blue, and it will be like showing up to your high school homecoming game wearing the other team's jersey. Big no-no."

She turned from Autumn and eyed the other women. "We're all going to wear red?"

"No, we're just not wearing blue." Sierra shoved an armful of dresses at her. "Try these. They will look beautiful."

Thirty minutes later and way too many dresses to count, Gwen walked out with her choice in hand. "I think I'm finally done." She looked around the empty space. Shoes and dresses were scattered everywhere as purses and coats all lay in a heap on the floor, long forgotten.

"Which one did you pick?" one of the girls questioned from her dressing room.

Gwen didn't answer. Her attention was drawn to Sierra and a man talking, off to the side of the boutique.

"Devon, I told you. I'm fine. I-I just need time for my brother and my dad to cool down. That's all.

"I don't understand. You told them you wouldn't let me go with you, right?"

Sierra looked to her toes. "I did, but I'm not sure they bought it."

"Why?"

The sharp edge to the man's voice had Gwen moving before she thought better of it. "Because neither of them would have put a woman, let alone *his* woman, in a cab when it was so *painfully* obvious she needed an ambulance. They sure as *hell* would not have sent her on her own."

Gwen couldn't tell if Sierra was happy to have her interfere or terrified by it. "Gwen, this is Devon. Devon, meet Gwen. She is one of the medics on my brother's shift and a very good friend of mine."

As she looked to the man who stood in front of her, Gwen would have said it was a completely different person from the one who spoke so harshly only a few seconds ago. Gone were the narrowed eyes and the hard lines of his face. In their place were bright, almost caring eyes with a smile that looked to be contagious and genuine.

"Gwen, it is so good to finally meet you. Sierra has told me so much about you."

A chameleon. That was the first thing that popped into her head. Changing its appearance in a blink of an eye to survive and thrive in any surrounding.

A chill ran up her spine as he grabbed the hand that hung loosely at the side of her body, shaking it as if they were meeting under any other circumstance. Had she not made her disdain toward him clear?

She roughly pulled her hand from his. "Sierra, are you okay?"

"I'm fine; I was just telling Devon that my family isn't all that thrilled with me right now."

"Good," Devon chimed in, taking Sierra's hand in his, his eyes going soft as he looked at her. She was almost able to hide the flinch. Almost. "When I came back into the room from retrieving her purse to find her gone, I could have paddled her little butt." He ran his hand down the side of her face. "But I was beyond relieved to hear that it was only a dislocation and not a break."

A battle raged inside her head. She wanted so badly to hold on to her dislike for the man, but the way his eyes got soft every time he looked at Sierra made it increasingly difficult. "I found you a dress for the ball that will look beautiful with your hair." Gwen looped her arm through her friend's, turning her in the direction of the dressing rooms before turning to the man. "It was nice to meet you."

"Absolutely. We will all have to get together for supper some night soon." Sincerity shone bright in his eyes, confusing the hell out of Gwen.

She forced herself to walk at a steady, normal pace as she moved toward her vacant dressing room. As soon as they were inside, she turned to the shaking girl in her arms. "Are you okay?"

"I'm fine, I-I just need a minute." Her sob tore her declaration to shreds.

"I'm calling the cops."

"No! The only thing calling the cops will accomplish is embarrassing me." She wiped at her eyes. "It's just…" She looked at her toes before looking Gwen straight in the eye. "…he isn't happy with me. I was supposed to wait for him, but when he was in the other room, I left and flagged down the first cab I saw. Now my family is mad at the both of us and ready to have a few choice words with him. This is not the first impression either of us wanted." She shook her head. "I'm in trouble, a lot of trouble, and not just with him."

It made sense. Hell, it had happened to her before. Mess up, break the rules, dread the consequences. It fit. She knew Sierra well, but did she know her kinks well enough to judge the conversation between the two of them?

"I am going to ask one question, and I need an honest answer." Sierra nodded. "Are you afraid of him?"

"God, no." Fingering her necklace, Sierra let a harsh laugh escape. "Maybe when he is wielding his paddle, but even that is my choice."

"Are you sure?"

"Unless he has an implement aimed at my ass, he is harmless." She paused for a second before adding, "It's not him I'm scared of."

Chapter 20

"I have good news."

"You caught both the arsonist and the copycat, and it turns out you were wrong this whole time and it wasn't an inside job?" Gwen attempted a sweet and innocent smile.

Atticus' eyes cut to the man at her side. "You have your hands full."

"Wouldn't have it any other way."

"While I would love nothing more than for the news to be just that, you know it's not. Nonetheless, your living quarters have all been swept, and you're in the clear." Cheers rang through the small group as glasses clicked together.

"Are you on shift?"

"Rare night off, actually."

"Then join us," Liv offered as she pushed the chair next to her out with the toe of her shoe.

"I would be happy to, lovie." He took the offered chair and threw his arm over the back of Liv's chair as he addressed the group. "Sierra decide to stay home tonight?"

"I am not sure decided is the correct word." The woman next to Leland smacked his chest lightly. "Princess," he warned.

"Don't embarrass her."

"I am going to embarrass you if you don't keep your hands to yourself." When she dropped her eyes, Leland continued. "She is staying with my parents, and this time, I spoke to my dad and know she is actually staying there, but Dad gave her the old 'my house, my rules' speech, so she is either nursing a sore butt or grounded."

"My bet is on the first one." As he stood from the table, Zander pulled out his darts. "Anyone up for kicking my ass in a game?"

When the door to the bar swung open an hour later, a strangled sound escaped Autumn. As she followed her line of sight, Gwen smiled and waved to the man. "I'm surprised to see him here. I didn't think he could be in a bar."

"It isn't a term of his probation," Kennly muttered absent mindedly. "But he doesn't drink, so."

"Autumn, we should…" She stopped short when she caught site of the woman sitting across from her. "Are you hiding?"

"No, I just…" She sat up straighter in her chair, avoiding eye contact with everyone.

"What did you do?" Kennly's whisper was ignored.

"Hey, Colt." Gwen's smile fell from her lips when the stormy look on the man's face registered.

Eyes glued to Autumn, his demand rumbled across the table, "Is your man here?"

"Umm." Her eyes shot to the dart board for just a second, but it was enough.

"Do not move." After issuing his order, he turned to the three stunned women. "Ladies."

"Colt."

"Can you do me a favor and keep her here for me? I'm sure Leland will want to talk to her when I am done talking to him." Without waiting for a response, he strolled away, leaving three gaping women in his wake.

"I'm dead."

"What did you do?" Liv asked, her eyes narrowed.

"I tried talking to Colt."

Gwen stared open mouthed at the woman. "You, what?"

"I tried to talk to Colt."

"Like, on the phone?"

"No, I—"

"Autumn Rose Johnson."

"Oh, fuck." Gwen watched as the other woman tracked her man's movements across the bar with her eyes. "I'm so dead."

When the group of guys stopped at the table, Atticus held his hand out to Liv. "I have no idea what's going on, but I have a feeling this is going to get a little heated, lovie. Care to join me for dinner?"

Without a second's hesitation, Liv laid her hand in his and allowed him to pull her from the chair. With a wide-eyed look and a wave over her shoulder, she followed him out of the bar.

"Tell me he is mistaken."

"He. I…" Her eyes dropped to her hands as she picked at her nails.

"I am waiting, Autumn, and my patience is running dangerously thin."

"He isn't lying, Sir."

"Did you know she was going to do this?"

Gwen looked at Jensen as he took his seat next to her, his whispered question catching her off guard. "No, I-I'm still not sure what she did."

"Tell them, Autumn."

"Sir."

"Now.

"I contacted Colt."

A snort from the man in question contradicted his hard look. "Contacted me? That implies that you picked up the phone and called me or sent a text. No, you showed up at my house. You talked to my mother, and then, the best part, you convinced her that you were a 'special friend' of mine."

"Well, our relationship is a little unconventional. Some would say special."

"I swear to God." Leland rested his clenched fist on the table, bringing his face down to Autumn's level so he could speak to her without the entire bar hearing him. "Livid. I am livid right now and far beyond the point where I can deal with this any time soon."

"I'm sorry, Sir."

"You will be, but for right now, you are going to sit right here, slip your panties out from under that skirt of yours and sit your naked ass on that chair."

"Sir?"

"Now. You know the rule. When my princess is naughty, she doesn't get her panties."

Gwen gave the other woman a sad but encouraging smile when their eyes met. The second of reassurance did the trick.

While dropping her eyes to the table, Autumn wiggled in her seat before she pushed off the chair, slipped her hands under her skirt and dragged her underwear down her bare legs in the middle of the crowded restaurant before fisting them in her hand. A blush colored her face when Leland held out his hand for the garment.

As soon as it dropped into his hand, he shoved them into his pants pocket and issued his final order, "Spread your legs, lift your skirt, and put your naked, disobedient ass on the chair." After a few seconds, the man's face softened. "Good girl. Stay here. I have a game to finish and some nerves to calm." He slapped Colt on the back and addressed the other man as they walked away. "Any good at darts?"

"I don't know; the prison system frowns on the inmates playing with sharp and pointy items."

Laughter faded as Gwen turned back to Autumn. "What were you thinking?"

"I was thinking that this all was taking too long. I just…I just wanted to see if he had any more information."

"You put this whole thing at risk!" Kennly's tone was harsh.

"I only went to talk to him."

"What if Atticus hadn't left? We decided not to tell the cops about Colt for a reason, and you nearly destroyed that."

"I know."

"She messed up; there's no reason for you to scold her, too. Leland will do plenty of that later."

"Can we talk about something else? Anything else. Please?"

It was silent for a second before a smile slowly spread across Kennly's face. "Did anyone else notice how eager Liv was to leave with Atticus?"

"Yes!"

"Wait, what?" Autumn asked.

"He asked her to dinner."

"A date? How did I miss this?"

"Probably had something to do with the group of men glaring daggers at you."

"I thought you were changing the subject."

Gwen stirred her drink before pushing it away as she chewed her lip. "Are they dating?"

"I don't know. I hope not." Shocked, both women turned to Kennly. "I mean, don't you think it's a little fast? Kevin hasn't been gone very long."

"There's more, isn't there?"

"I don't know. I just can't read the guy, and I don't like that."

Sierra reached across the table and patted Kennly's hand. "I don't think they're dating, I think he feels for her, like he knows what it feels like to lose someone like she did. Give him a chance."

"Hell, he's working harder to catch the arsonist than Starling ever did, even before it was his case."

"You're right."

"Autumn." Her name was all the instruction she needed. With bottom lip caught between her teeth, Autumn stood from the table and allowed Leland to lead her from the bar.

"Is he going to do what I think he is?"

As she allowed the corner of her mouth to quirk, Gwen turned to Colt. "Do you think he's going to bare her ass and make her regret breaking a promise?" At his nod, she continued. "Then, yeah, he is going to do exactly what you think he is."

Chapter 21

"We have a report of a man down at the corner of Plymouth and Frank." Gwen pried her eyes open, glancing at the red numbers glowing from the clock. 0343. Too early. She stood from her bed, shoved her feet into her boots, grabbed her radio off the nightstand and was headed to the bay as she shrugged on her jacket.

"What are you doing up?" she questioned the man standing in his socks next to the rig.

"Is a man not allowed to kiss his girl before she leaves?"

"Not when she is leaving before four in the morning."

"Davis was sick; I just sent him home." When she went to climb into the rig, he took hold of her chin, catching her eyes for the briefest moment before planting a hard kiss on her lips. "Be safe." She watched him walk away.

"Quit ogling the man. We have a patient who needs us."

"I am allowed to stare at his ass; he's mine after all." The bay door opened and she pulled forward and flipped on the lights as she pulled into the road. "You want me to take lead on this, or do you want it?"

"It's mine. You had the last one."

Gwen glanced to her partner as she maneuvered around a car that had pulled over to accommodate the ambulance. "What's wrong?"

"Nothing is wrong." A smile spread across Autumn's face. "Leland asked me to move in with him."

"Oh my God! I would give you a hug if it wouldn't kill the both of us. When?"

"He mentioned it the other night after he found out about and dealt with the whole Colt thing. Said it would help him to keep a better eye on me." She pointed to the road. "That idiot isn't going to move. When I was helping him wash the trucks, earlier tonight, he brought it up again."

A flick of a switch had the sirens wailing. "Nothing says romance like physical labor, but hell, at least you weren't draped over his thighs for this conversation."

"A romantic he is not, but I don't need romance. I just need Lee."

"Ahh." In an attempt to get the infuriating truck to move, Gwen hit the horn impatiently before she put her hand over her heart.

Her teasing gesture turned into a scream as the truck in front of them stomped on its brakes, swerving dangerously before screeching to a halt in the middle of the road, blocking both lanes of traffic. As she hit her own breaks, Gwen was able to bring the ambulance to a stop before they were in an accident. "Holy shit!"

"Ambulance 23 to dispatch."

"Go ahead, Ambulance 23."

"We are at the corner of—" There was a heavy tap on the window.

"Put the mic down, Autumn." When the woman hesitated, the masked man pulled Sierra roughly into view from the side of the rig. "Do it, or I shoot her." Gwen's eyes landed on the gun that had been used to knock on the window, noticing it for the first time.

"Ambulance 23, you were cut off, can you repeat your last transmission?"

"Jay, I—" That was all the further Sierra got before the man released her arm and backhanded her across the face.

"I told you to shut up!"

Gwen's door was pulled open and a hand wrapped around her arm. She cried as she was pulled from the rig and into another man's arms. "Devon?"

"Do as you're told, and you won't get hurt. Cause a scene, and I can't protect you." He nodded to the other man and continued. "He will make Jensen's punishments look like child's play." He grabbed for her radio, pulling it from her belt and holding it up to her mouth. "Tell dispatch that you're at the scene. Tell them!"

"Ambulance 23 to dispatch. We're on scene."

Chapter 22

"Firefighter Davis to Dispatch." The frantic tone in the man's voice had Jensen on his feet, his heart in his throat.

"Go ahead, Firefighter Davis."

"I just rolled up on ambulance 23. It's abandoned." Breathing instantly became difficult.

"Repeat that, Firefighter Davis."

"I rolled up on Ambulance 23. The doors are open, the radios are here, but the paramedics are gone.

"What do you mean, you don't know where they are? There are cameras on the inside and the outside of the rig. Use them."

"We tried, but the devices were scrambled."

"Meaning what?"

"The recordings are useless. The only thing we have is six minutes of static."

"The radios worked; I heard the girls call in before Davis got there."

"The radios use older technology. The people who did this knew that, and they used it to their advantage. They needed a head start. Thankfully, Davis came upon the scene, or who knows how long it would have taken before anyone realized they never made it to the call. Truthfully, they never should have radioed that they were there."

Jensen took a threatening step toward the officer. "Don't question the choices of my people."

"Don't threaten my men. They can only tell you what they know."

"Then tell me you have more information! Tell me you know where the girls are."

Atticus shook his head slowly. "I don't have any other material to give you."

"Sir." An officer walked up to the small group of men, leaning in to speak privately with his superior.

"What is it?"

"A street cam caught a truck headed out of town."

"Was it the girls?"

He nodded his head, briefly closing his eyes as he took a deep breath. "One of them was able to jump from the car."

"Who?"

"Autumn."

Liv stepped out of the curtained off section of the ER and was immediately surrounded by a handful of men.

"How is she?"

"She just got here, but she looks fine, a few bumps and bruises, maybe a minor concussion, but nothing major that I can see so far." Leland didn't need any more information before he disappeared behind the wall of fabric. Jensen looked to the small woman. "Even if I say no, you are still going to barge in there and ask her a million questions. Go, get it over with so she can rest." When he went to step away, she grabbed his arm. "Get our girls home safe."

As soon as he stepped into the space, a broken cry hit his ears. "I'm sorry. I didn't want to leave them, but the door on the other side was broken and he sat between us."

"Calm down, princess."

"What happened?"

"We had no choice."

"I know, but we still need you to tell us what happened."

"The truck. It stopped in front of us. Gwen tried to call it in, but they were at the door before she could tell dispatch what happened. We had no choice. They had Sierra."

"Fuck!" Atticus pulled his phone from his pocket and sent out a quick text. "Tell us anything you remember, lovie, even if you think it is useless. The tiniest clue could get us on the right path."

"Gwen knew the guy who pulled her from the rig, called him Devon. I recognized the other one's voice, but his face was covered and I can't place it."

"If you heard it again, would you know it?" At her frantic nod, Atticus hit a few buttons on his phone before a voicemail started playing.

"That's it, that's who pulled me out of the ambulance."

Jensen felt his mouth drop as realization hit. "Starling's the arsonist?"

Atticus scuffed. "No, he's the copycat. Did they say anything about where they were going, or what they were going to do? Were there more people waiting for them to arrive?"

"They did say they had one more stop to make."

"Did they say where?"

"No. It was something about picking up a 'pretty pig.'"

Jensen watched as Zander shot from his chair, the color gone from his face. "Baylor." He pulled his phone from his pocket. "Fuck! Little bird, I swear to God, if you're screening your calls or your phone is dead, I am going to paddle your ass. Pick up the phone. Please, baby."

"I need a location on Officer Bass right now."

Chapter 23

Gwen silently pleaded for the unconscious woman on the floor in front of her to wake up. The bleeding had stopped, but the ugly blue and purple knot near her temple had her worried.

"You didn't have to hurt her."

"She didn't do as she was told."

"Is that what happened to Sierra's arm. Did she not react to your command fast enough?"

"That was an accident! I would never hurt her on purpose." The younger man swiftly moved across the room. Sierra flinched away as he brought his hand to her face, brushing against the bruise that had formed as a result of the earlier backhand. "You believe me, don't you, baby?"

"Of c-course."

"Get back to the fucking window."

Gwen's stomach recoiled as the man next to her removed his ski mask. "Starling?"

"Did you expect the boogie man?" He mopped his sweaty face with his sleeve, making sure to be gentle with his swollen eye.

"You're the arsonist?" The slap had her falling from her

kneeling position to her side, her tied hands unable to brace her fall.

"That is the problem." He leaned into her, his breath smelling of stale cigarettes. "Everyone was so wrapped up in him that they forgot all about me. I was old news; I couldn't have that."

"What did you do to be remembered?"

She cringed away when Starling raised his hand to strike her again, but it never came. When she opened her eyes, she saw Devon holding the other man's wrist. "You said you wouldn't hurt them unless they disobeyed. All she did was ask a question." He released Starling and walked back to the window, his blue eyes flashing. Gwen could see why Sierra had been drawn to him. He was a protector, even if he was a bit deranged. As she looked at the other woman now, all she could see was disdain mixed with just a hint of fear every time she snuck a glance at him.

A sneer curled Starling's lip. "You mean, besides giving the last ten years of my life to protecting this city? How about taking Devon, here, off the streets, giving him a place to live and food to eat."

"And turning him into a monster like you," Sierra cried out as her head was pulled back by a fist in her hair.

"Sounds like you need a lesson in who's in charge."

"No." Devon stepped forward, a deadly look on his face. "She is mine; I will handle her."

Starling was a lot of things, but it didn't seem he was as big an idiot as Gwen had previously thought. "Fine." He shoved Sierra to the floor, forcing her to her hands and knees in front of Devon. "Make sure she doesn't disrespect me again, or I will tie and gag her whether you agree or not."

He crouched in front of her, gently touching her chin so she looked him in the eye. "You know better than to disrespect him like that. You know he doesn't like it, and I hate punishing you."

"I…" Fear rolled off of her. "I hate him. He's turned you into a monster."

"It's not her fault, Devon." Gwen spoke as she struggled into a seated position. "She's terrified, not just for herself, but for us."

He instantly softened. "Is that true?"

"Bullshit."

"Shut up, Jay. Let her talk."

Sierra looked to the floor as she clenched her fist so tightly, her knuckles turned white. An attempt to keep herself from slugging the man, no doubt. "You kidnapped me and my friends."

"Oh, baby." She held herself stiff as he gathered her in his arms.

"You're going to fall for that shit?"

"We're holding her here against her will, for reasons unknown to her. Of course, she's scared."

"They are playing you!"

When Jay took a step toward Sierra, Devon stood to his full height. "Let me get them all settled in the bedroom." Devon helped both women off the floor and led them to what looked to be the only other room in the house. "Stay here and behave. I don't want to have to punish you, but I will if you give me a reason."

He left the room, only to return a second later with Kennly's limp form cradled in his arms. He placed her on the bed, gave Sierra's hand a kiss and walked out the room, locking the door from the outside.

As she caught Gwen's eye, Sierra spoke. "I'm not afraid of him. I'm scared of Starling and the beast he has turned Devon into."

"Are they gone?"

"Thank God!"

"Shh." Kennly sat up, stretching her arms above her head. "If they know I'm conscious, they'll tie me, and we need as many free hands as we can get." She started working the knots holding

Gwen's wrists as she spoke. "My name is Baylor Bass. I'm an undercover police officer for the Hill City Police Department."

"What?" Gwen looked over her shoulder to the woman working the knots holding her hands.

"I'm an undercover cop."

"That's why they called you a—" Gwen stopped, not wanting to insult the woman.

"I can only imagine what they call me, but we don't have time." Baylor turned to Sierra. "I need to know what happened."

"I don't know. I was in the grocery store parking lot, and then I was here. When I woke up, Jay was mad. Said he had to teach me a lesson." Her audible gulp had Gwen reaching for her hand with her now freed one. "He…I fought him as much as I could, but he still got my pants down. Devon, thank goodness, got back from the outhouse as I was fighting to keep my underwear. He pulled me away from Jay and punched him all in the same second."

"The black eye?"

"Yeah, that's from Devon."

"What time were you at the grocery store?"

"Late evening. Eight, maybe."

"Good."

Sierra looked to the floor. "They made me text my parents. They're probably mad at me for not coming home, but I doubt they sent out a search team."

"But that gives us a timeline."

Gwen straightened her spine, smiling. "They'll understand. Even if they aren't looking for you, we left a completely stocked rig in the middle of a busy intersection. Someone will call it in. Then there's Autumn; she'll tell the guys."

Kennly stood and started looking around the room. "We are going to need weapons. Let's see what we can find."

"Do you understand the plan?"

"I don't like it." Sierra picked at the peeling paint of the lamp she held in her hands.

Kennly's face grew hard as she pressed her ear to the door. After a few seconds, she responded in a harsh whisper. "It's a simple plan, but we don't have a choice. You heard them. They're making plans to move us further away from Hill City and the people who are looking for us. I will *not* let that happen."

"But—"

Gwen crossed the room to the terrified woman. "Sierra, we have to do this; it is the only way all of us will get out."

"But the window."

"They would hear the glass shattering. One, maybe two of us would get out, but not all of us."

"Then I'll distract them. You two get out."

"Wait." Taking a page out of Jensen's book, Gwen took hold of Sierra's chin and forced the other woman to look her in the eyes. "Do you want to stay here?"

"No, but if my staying here gets the two of you out, I am more than willing."

"Are you kidding?"

"Hear me out."

"No, it's my job to protect you two, and I am damn well going to do it."

Sierra scuffed at Kennly. "I may be a little, but I am not a child."

"That's not what I meant."

Sierra didn't give the other woman a chance to explain. "We listened to you; now you're going to listen to me." When the other woman said nothing, Sierra took a deep breath and continued. "Devon may be deranged, but he wouldn't hurt me or let Jay get his hands on me. He's proven that twice. I feel stupid holding this thing." She set the lamp down on the bed. "Look, it's my fault the two of you are here. Let me be the reason you get out. I can keep them back long enough for both of you to get out the window."

Gwen willed her voice not to shake. "We don't know where we are, Sierra. By the time we get help, you could be long gone. I'm not willing to risk that."

After a shaky breath, Sierra shook her head and picked up the lamp again. "Okay. I'll do it."

Back in position, Gwen met each woman's eyes. This was going to go one of two ways. As planned or horribly wrong.

Kennly listened intently. "Starling just left. Wait. Wait." As she took a step back from the door, Kennly nodded at Sierra.

The lamp shattered against the hardwood floor a second before Sierra's scream bounced off the walls. Within moments, Devon barreled through the door. He didn't get any further before Gwen threw the long forgotten bottle of perfume in his face.

He roared in agony when the smelly contents hit his face, bathing his eyes in the harsh chemicals. When he instinctively covered his face with his hands, Kennly stepped forward, landing a kick to his balls before wrenching his arm behind his back and forcing him into the closet.

As soon as she got the chair wedged under the door, they ran through the cabin, out the front door, and into the snow. Gwen breathed a sigh of relief. They had made it!

Sierra's scream halted her in her tracks. Gwen turned just in time to see Kennly take a flying leap at Starling, landing on his back. The three of them fell in a heap on the ground, Sierra a few feet from the others.

"Run!" Neither woman moved to do as Kennly demanded.

Starling got to his feet with the woman still in place, arms and legs anchoring her to him. She cried out in pain when he reached back and raked his nails up her shoulders, leaving parallel lines in his wake, blood slowly seeping from the wounds.

"Motherfucker!" The sound of her thumbs pushing into the

man's eyes was disgusting, but it did the job. In his frantic attempts to save his sight, he dropped the cell phone he held. "Take the phone and run!"

The desperation in the other woman's voice propelled Gwen into action. She grabbed the phone from the ground and took Sierra's hand, pulling her further away from the fight.

"Fucking bitch," Starling roared as he turned and backed into the wall of the cabin, slamming Kennly into the unrelenting surface.

"There's no service."

"Run," Kennly wheezed as she fell from Starling's back and his booted foot kicked her in the ribs. She curled into herself. "Please, just run." Another kick had her screaming in pain and Gwen on her feet.

Chapter 24

"They are going to find them."

"When? When it is too late?" Jensen paced the length of the small space. "Twelve hours. It has been twelve hours since anyone has seen her. They could be anywhere."

"Or they could be right under our noses."

"Then, where are they?" He dropped into a chair, his head fell back and he glared at the ceiling. "Where is she?"

How in the hell did this woman become so important to him is such a short amount of time? He had known and worked alongside her for years, but somehow, in just a few short months, she had managed to worm her way into his heart and become so much more than a coworker.

"I should have stayed with them. I could have helped."

"Then we would be looking for four women rather than three." All eyes swung to Atticus as he pushed past the curtain. "I just got confirmation. A neighbor saw a truck fitting the description of the one we are looking for in front of her house early this morning. They have Baylor."

Zander ran his hands over his hair. "I should have made her come to the station. I should have made sure she was safe."

"Why didn't you tell us about Kennly?"

"Baylor." He collapsed into a chair, the cheap metal creaking under his weight. "I wanted to tell you, but she was worried she would lose her job. Her last three cases haven't gone well, and she was told if she messed this one up, both her job and endorsement would be gone."

Jensen growled as he stood from his chair and towered over Zander's sitting form. "I let her go into burning buildings without the proper training!"

"She's trained. She went through fire school, was recruited from there by PD and went to the police academy. When her last op went bad, she applied for a position with us. When PD found out, they promised her a probationary position at the station of her choice, as soon as she was done with this case."

"She get that in writing?"

"Signed by the mayor."

Mollified a bit, Jensen took his seat. "She'll be staying with us when this is all said and done?"

"Damn right; she'll be lucky if I ever let her out of my sight again."

The ringing phone kept anyone from responding. "This is Keetes."

"Jensen?"

"Fuck, Gwendolyn, tell me where you are. I'll come get you."

Her heavy breathing broke up her response. "The plan. We were all supposed to get out. It didn't work. I don't think he went all the way to the outhouse."

"What didn't work? Where are you?" He hit speaker, filling the room with the sound of labored breathing and snow crunching beneath feet. "Tell us you're okay!"

"Sierra and I are running through the woods."

"Where's Ba-Kennly?"

"Kennly? She's still in the cabin. We were all supposed to get out, but he came out of nowhere. She poked him in the eyes and he dropped the phone. She was supposed to come with us."

"Fuck!" Zander's roar echoed off the walls. "Tell us where you are!"

"I don't know!"

Jensen looked to the officer. "Atticus, can you trace this?

Phone in hand, he replied, "I'm already on it."

"Gwen." Her crying was twisting his heart in a knot. "Bellissima, I need you to stay on the line."

"The service is shit, but I'll try, Sir."

"Are they following you?"

"You want me to look back? You never look back! Every person who has ever looked back in the history of scary movies has died. It's like running away from bad guys 101."

"Gwendolyn, focus. Are you being followed?"

"If I turn around and he's right behind me, I am blaming you." There was a pause. "No. No one is following us."

"Can you see the cabin?".

"Yes."

"Don't move. Stay there, watch the cabin and tell us what you remember about the trip there."

"I remember the lights."

"Lights?"

"Our lights. We passed our spot not long before we got to the cabin."

"Good girl. Anything else, baby?"

The sound of a scream echoed through the phone's speaker. "Kennly! Kennly!"

The beep indicating the call had ended was deafening.

"I have it narrowed down, but it's a five-mile radius. My guys and I are on it."

As soon as Atticus was out the door, Zander turned to Jensen.

"They're hurting her; we don't have that kind of time. I know you have a better idea of where they are." Zander's look of panic had Jensen's anger rocketing up a notch.

"They're near the *Land of a Thousand Stars*." As he pocketed his phone, he looked to his brothers. "Let's go."

Chapter 25

Having to wait for her friend's scream to cover the sound of the breaking glass was heartbreaking, but it worked. They were now standing at the closet door. "Are you sure this is going to work?"

"No, but I am willing to give it a shot." With a deep breath, she knocked three times. "Daddy?"

"Baby, are you okay? You scared me."

"I know. I'm sorry, but we were so scared."

"You are in so much trouble."

"I know, but I—we—need your help."

A long sigh floated to their ears. "All you had to do was listen, and everything would have been fine."

"You know that isn't true. You know how twisted he is."

The silence was thick as the seconds ticked by. Finally, Devon spoke. "I know."

"I need your help. He's hurting her, and the only one who can stop him is you."

A scream pierced the air. "I'm not so sure about that."

"You kept him from hurting me twice since we got here. You can stop him." Sierra swallowed hard before she continued, her face twisted as if the words tasted bitter on her tongue. "I know you can, Daddy."

"Let me out, baby. I'll save your friend."

When she reached for the chair, Gwen halted her. "Are you sure about this?"

"He loves me. In a twisted, not quite right in the head kind of way, but it's love nonetheless. He will help."

As soon as the door was open, Sierra was gathered in the man's arms. "I am so glad you're all right." He pushed her back so he could get a good look at her.

A scream from the other room had Gwen moving. "Please. I don't know what he's doing to her, but you have to stop him."

Devon nodded and looked Sierra in the eye. "Stay out of the way. I don't want you getting hurt." As soon as he got the agreement he needed, Devon swung the door opened and made his way across the small room.

The sight before her had Gwen's heart dropping to her toes. Kennly lay on her back, her arms tied to the post in the middle of the room, her shirt sliced down the middle and pushed to the side. Starling sat on top of her, knife in hand, and a crazed expression on his face as he pulled the tip of the knife across her abdomen. Blood ran in rivulets down her flat tummy soaking the waist band of her pants and trickling to the floor, her mouth open in a silent scream.

"What the fuck!" Devon's voice was hard as steel as he shoved the other man to the ground and off the now sobbing woman.

Before she realized she was moving, Gwen was kneeling beside her friend frantically working at the knots. "We're going to get you out of here. I promise."

"Why didn't— You were supposed to run."

Taking note of her shallow breaths, she smiled at the injured woman. "And let you have all the fun? Not a chance."

"Did you?"

"I talked to Jensen. They're coming." As the knot loosened

beneath her fingers, Gwen sent a silent prayer to whoever was listening. *Please let them be fast enough.* With the knot undone, Kennly's arms fell to the floor with an audible thud.

A pained grunt caught Gwen's attention. When she looked up, she watched the shiny, silver blade sink into Devon's thigh. "This is what happens when you bite the hand that feeds you!" He pulled the knife from its resting place and Starling slashed at the other man's chest, leaving a thin line of blood in its wake.

"Feeds me? You manipulated and used me. You promised not to hurt them. You said you were helping them."

"Help me move her." As Sierra moved to help, Gwen looked to her injured friend. "Your broken ribs are going to make any movement excruciating, but I need you to be as quiet as possible." She looked to the fighting men. "They've forgotten we're here, and we need to keep it that way."

"Gag me. I'm lying still, and I already want to scream. It will be the only way," Kennly said.

Gwen slipped off what was left of Kennly's shirt and wadded it into a ball. "Are you ready?"

"Promise me, if I'm too loud, you'll run."

"Never."

Before the argument could slip past her lips, Gwen pushed the balled-up shirt into her mouth and took her place next to Sierra. "We're moving her to the bedroom and locking ourselves in with the chair. It should buy us enough time to get out the window. As soon as we get to the bedroom, I will block the door and you take the gag out of her mouth. She's struggling enough without the gag; she'll suffocate if it's there too long. On three. One. Two. Three!"

A scream sounded behind the impromptu gag, the instant they started moving her. "Don't stop, Sierra. Keep going. We're almost there."

"But, you're not going to make it." A fist took hold of Gwen's hair, pulling her back and forcing her to drop Kennly. Another scream sounded before Kennly went limp.

As she struggled against the hold, she turned to Sierra. "The gag." That was all she was able to say before something cold, wet, and hard was pressed against her throat. The knife.

"Any more fucking tricks, and I slice her throat. Don't move."

"She can't breathe," Sierra cried as she looked to the woman who was passed out in front of her.

"I don't fucking care! One more fucking step, and she won't be the only one who can't breathe."

"Okay." Raising her hands above her head, she stepped away from Kennly.

"See, Devon, this is how you get your 'baby' to do as she is told."

Gwen searched for the man without moving and came up empty. "He's not here."

"What?"

She felt the knife glide ever so slightly across her throat as she turned. The stinging confirmed her fear. He had cut her. She combatted her rising panic and took stock of herself. She was still able to breathe, no lightheadedness. Only a nick, but he was being careless.

Movement caught her attention as Sierra stepped in front of them, her arms still in the air. "I… He left me?" Tears fell from her eyes. "How could he?"

"Shut up! I can't think with your blubbering."

"You're outnumbered, Starling. You can't control both of us."

"Shut up."

Ignoring his command, Gwen continued, hoping her hunch was right and she would be able to buy some time. "He left you here to take the fall, and now it's three against one."

"I swear, if you don't stop talking right now, I am going to even out the odds."

"I have to find him," Sierra wailed as she ran for the door.

"No!" As soon as the knife left her throat, everything happened in slow motion.

Going limp, Gwen was able to slip from his hold, land on her knees, and crawl a few feet away. When he realized his mistake, Starling turned around and was met with a cast iron frying pan to the face before falling to the ground, unconscious.

Chapter 26

"Jensen?"

"Gwen, are you okay?"

A harsh laugh filled the empty forest. "I don't know if I would say okay, but I'm not dead."

Bile filled his throat as he took in the state of her throat. "I'm going to kill him."

"Will you settle for maimed?" She nodded toward the house. "He took a skillet to the face, courtesy of Kennly… or Baylor. He's now comatose and tied to a chair."

As he pushed his girl behind him, he said into his mic, "I've got Gwen."

"Jensen, you're not listening. We got them. Well, one of them."

"Where's the other?"

"I don't know; he ran after Starling stabbed him."

"Thank God." He gathered his woman in his arms and pressed the mic again. "The girls took Starling out with a frying pan."

Laughter sounded behind them before a pained moan took over. "Fuck, don't make me laugh. Broken ribs, remember?"

"Baylor, baby?" Zander emerged from the tree line.

"Don't," both women yelled as he went to wrap his arms around her.

"I took a couple of kicks to the ribs. I'll be fine, but it will take a while."

"Fuck, little bird, you had me worried." He grabbed her face between his hands, careful of the goose egg near her temple, and gave the crown of her head a kiss.

"I'll be fine, Z."

"She's strong."

"And bull headed."

"Sierra? Thank fuck!" Leland gathered his little sister in his arms.

"You're a little late to the party, big brother. We had to do all the heavy lifting ourselves." Her voice broke on the last word, and in a second, she was sobbing in Leland's arms.

"I'm sorry."

"It wasn't your fault, Cici."

"I trusted a monster. Fuck, I fell in love with a monster."

"Did Atticus read you the riot act about interfering in police business?"

"I'm pretty sure his blood pressure hit an all new high."

Gwen, smiling at him from his bed, had his cock twitching. "Doesn't bode well for when we tell him about Colt."

A smirk hitched the corner of his mouth. "Maybe we will keep that one between us for a while."

"All six of us?" His eyes shifted to the bandage at her throat. "It's just a nick. Not even close to anything important."

"He could have killed you." His gut twisted into a knot just thinking of the other possible outcomes.

"He didn't. Instead, he's in the ICU with a brain bleed, fighting for his life."

"He's lucky Atticus and his guys showed up before I was able to pry myself from your arms. He'd be in the morgue."

"Still a good chance he'll end up there. Kennly, er, Baylor has some major power behind her swing."

He climbed into bed, chuckling as he replied, "It's going to take a while to get used to calling her that."

"I think it fits her better." Her eyes sliding down his body had his cock jumping again. "You're driving me crazy, bellissima."

"Then come do something about it."

"You sure?"

Her shrug caused her unruly curls to fall into her face. "I mean, if you're afraid I'm too fragile." She sat up a bit, the movement allowing the covers to slip, exposing her naked chest. Hands traveled to her breast, her fingers pulled at the rings, extracting a long, drawn out moan, before one of her hands slid below the blankets. "I can always take care of things myself."

He caught her hand before it got too far and growled, "Mine."

"Prove it."

His lips were on hers before he knew what he was doing, his tongue gliding along the seam of her lips, diving into her mouth when she finally opened to him. After a few minutes, he pulled away, enjoying her whine of protest. "Shh. I'm not going anywhere."

As she wound her arms around his neck, she pulled him closer. "Could have fooled me, Sir."

"No." He smiled at her before running the tip of his finger gently across the small bandage at her neck. "Tonight, I need us to be us. Jensen and Gwen. Can we do that?"

"So I can kiss, touch, lick and bite you any time I want?"

"Absolutely."

"Jensen, make love to me?"

"With pleasure."

Without wasting a second, he captured her lips once more before moving down her body and landing a single kiss on the reminder of how the day could have gone.

Chapter 27

"May I have your attention please?"

"Jensen, what are you doing?" She reached for the butter knife he was clicking against his beer mug.

"What I should have done months ago. Attention, please." As the conversation around them dwindled, Gwen's face ignited in a beautiful blush. Jensen stood and held out a hand for her. "Bellissima, join me?"

Not even considering telling him no, she placed her hand in his and allowed him to drag her to the front of the room. "What are you doing?" Her whisper was a little harsher than she planned it to be.

He leaned in so only she could hear and replied, "If you're not careful, I am going to be tanning your ass as soon as I can find a quiet place. And to think, I had such fun plans for that ass later." As he caught her eyes with his, he let his brow raise in question. When her mouth snapped shut, he smiled. "That's what I thought." The chuckles of the few people close enough to hear his last remark floated to her ears.

As he then turned to the group in front of them, he smiled.

"Most of you are probably wondering what the hell I am doing up here. I know she is." The smile he shot Gwen's way had her rolling her eyes. "Bellissima."

"Yes, Sir?"

"Always a professional!" one of the men from another shift yelled, causing an uproar of laughter.

"If he only knew." His smoldering look had her core melting.

"Are you going to get on with the speech, or you going to stand up there all night?"

"First, I want to thank you all for coming to this year's Fireman's Ball. I know the people who put this together put a lot of work into it." He sought out Liv in the crowded room and smiled as he continued. "And Kevin would be happy to see all of us here, supporting his wife and honoring his memory. Second, I want to let all the women here know that they are all absolutely stunning." Gwen looked down at her black dress, the fabric falling to the floor and clinging to her curves. The slit on the side that rose to mid-thigh was the only reason she was able to walk in it.

"The real reason I came up here was to tell you a story. A month ago, four of our own were kidnapped by a man none of us liked, but we never thought he was capable of that level of evil." A sad smile spread across the man's face, his regret clear. "Thirty days ago, my brothers and I found our girls in an abandoned cabin, having already saved themselves. With a frying pan, no less. Thirty days ago, I realized that life was far too short to wait any longer. It was then that I decided I was going to marry this beautiful, strong woman."

Gwen's mouth dropped open as Jensen sank to one knee in front of her. "What are you doing?"

His dopey smile was back. "Proposing, bellissima."

"But why?" At his questioning look, she went on to explain, her voice a whisper, "You don't ask, Sir. You tell."

"Okay." He stood back up, opened the previously unnoticed

box, pulled the beautiful ring from its resting place and slid it on her finger before he pulled her into his arms. "Thirty days ago, I decided I was going to marry this woman, and next month, I will be doing just that."

"Next month, Sir?"

"Are you ever going to stop whispering?" He landed a kiss to the top of her head as she nodded. "Yes, a month. That's enough time to plan the necessary things and screw the rest. If I learned anything in those thirteen hours you were gone, it was that life is too short to wait. I want you as my wife, and I want it as soon as possible."

With a tear running down her face, she turned to the crowd that consisted of firefighters, medics and their spouses. Their people. Some, she knew well, others, she didn't, but it didn't matter; they were their people. "A month."

Cheers erupted around them as he lifted her from the floor with his hands on her ass and planted a heavy kiss on her lips. "You're going to be mine forever, little medic."

"I know, Sir."

"God, I can't wait."

Epilogue

Who knew? All it would take to get into their good graces was a single good deed. A spur of the moment decision. A few strategically wasted minutes. He was one of them. No longer an outsider.

Months of planning and strategizing had nearly gone to waste when the copycat made his appearance, but in the end, he ended up deeper into the fold than he ever thought he would. All thanks to Starling. It was too bad that he had to be taken care of. He was such an asset. Even if he was a pain in the ass.

As he stood from the table, a small hand wrapped around his forearm. "Don't leave yet.

"Trust me; no one leaves the Fireman's Ball this early, just stretching my legs. I'll be right back."

He turned toward the door, his lip raised in a snarl. She wasn't one of his girls. She was a wanna be. She lacked the finesse of his girls. The poise. Their fire. For now, she was what he had to settle for.

Once outside, he grabbed the ever present lighter from his pocket. The excitement of watching the hot, minute, crimson ember as it burned the white stick to a stub was too much to resist. Inhaling made him cough, as it always did, but the power he held between his fingers was too much to resist.

Power. A single misplaced or perfectly placed coal held such possibilities.

The need to burn something bigger was starting to mount. He could sense it like a bag of rocks in the pit of his stomach, growing heavier with every passing second.

He pushed the feeling aside and looked through the window. Smiles on every one of their faces. Their eyes glowing. The spark. It's what drew him to them in the first place, because it reminded him so much of her.

The fist tightened around his heart, making it hard for him to breath. Guilt.

He would be damned if he let theirs go out as hers did.

Another inhale, another coughing fit.

"I'm on to you."

As he spun on his heels, he came face to face with Baylor. "I'm sorry?"

"Come out here to smoke a cigarette that makes you cough every time you take a puff." She pulled out her own pack, flicking her lighter and setting the thin stick ablaze. "I'm trying to quit, too. Z says I'm too pretty for such a nasty habit." Her eyes never left his as she took a long drag. seeming to look into his soul. "It's a need, really. Watching the cherry burn the cigarette to nothing. Satisfying."

"He's right." As he plucked the offending object from between her lips, he tossed it to the pavement and ground it in with the heel of his shoe, trying his hardest not to let the panic show. Her words so closely echoed the thoughts that had run through his head. "Go back inside before you get yourself in trouble."

She simply smiled. "You're probably right. Can't risk getting caught, not with the promised consequences."

Did she see his secrets? His guilt? How much he wished to go back and change so many things? Did she know who he was, or was his mind simply toying with him?

He took another drag and knew it was time. The last fire had appeased the need to burn for a while, but it wouldn't hold for much longer. The media didn't care about him any longer. A tragic story thrown to the sidelines for some bigwig who'd made a touchdown, but with the copycat gone, it was time for the city's focus to shift back to him and his work. It already had, but it was with reports that the real Hill City arsonist had gone into hiding.

No hiding, never hiding. Just waiting in the dark until the need overcame him again.

"About time to remind everyone that I am still here."

The End

Rachel Blake

I have been writing since high school, but truthfully never thought it would go any further than a few short stories hidden deep within my laptop. It wasn't until my family moved away from everything we knew that I started writing stories worth sharing. Now, my husband, three kids, our plethora of animals and I live in the Midwest. When I'm not running around like your stereotypical soccer mom (sans the minivan) I am writing the type of stories I have always secretly treasured: love stories with a sexy alpha and a strong submissive counterpart.

Follow her here:
https://www.facebook.com/AuthorRachelBlake
https://www.instagram.com/rachelblakeauthor/
http://www.amazon.com/author/authorrachelblake

Don't miss these exciting titles by Rachel Blake and Blushing Books!

Hill City Heroes
Fire Princess - Book One
Beautiful Burn - Book Two

Milton Keynes UK
Ingram Content Group UK Ltd.
UKHW010012281223
435071UK00001B/31

9 781645 631804